A MILLIONAIRE
FOR CINDERELLA

BY

BARBARA WALLACE

MILLS
BOON®

publisher in any form of binding or cover other than that in which it is published and without a similar condition including this condition being imposed on the subsequent purchaser.

® and TM are trademarks owned and used by the trademark owner and/or its licensee. Trademarks marked with ® are registered with the United Kingdom Patent Office and/or the Office for Harmonisation in the Internal Market and in other countries.

First published in Great Britain 2015
by Mills & Boon, an imprint of Harlequin (UK) Limited,
Large Print edition 2015
Eton House, 18-24 Paradise Road,
Richmond, Surrey, TW9 1SR

© 2015 Barbara Wallace

ISBN: 978-0-263-25690-1

Harlequin (UK) Limited's policy is to use papers that are natural, renewable and recyclable products and made from wood grown in sustainable forests. The logging and manufacturing processes conform to the legal environmental regulations of the country of origin.

Printed and bound in Great Britain
by CPI Antony Rowe, Chippenham, Wiltshire

To Peter, who has the patience of a saint come deadline time, and to the revitalizing powers of coffee and snack-sized candy bars.

I never would have written this book if not for you all.

CHAPTER ONE

HOW LONG DID it take to examine one little old lady? Patience paced the length of the hospital emergency room for what felt like the hundredth time. What was taking so long?

"Excuse me." She knocked on the glass window separating the admissions desk from the rest of the emergency waiting area. "My...grandmother...has been back there for a long time." She figured the lie would get her more sympathy than saying "my employer." Luckily there'd been a shift change; the previous nurse on duty would have called her on it. "Is there any way I can find out what's happening?"

The nurse gave her a sympathetic smile. "I'm sorry, we're really busy today, and things are backed up. I'm sure a doctor will be out to talk with you soon."

Easy for her to say. She hadn't found her employer crumpled at the foot of a stairwell.

Ana's cry replayed in her head. Frail, weak. If only she hadn't been in the other room…if only she hadn't told Nigel he needed to wait for his dinner, then Ana wouldn't be here. She'd be having her tea in the main salon like she did every afternoon.

Patience couldn't help her sad, soft chuckle. A year ago she didn't know what a salon was. Goes to show how much working for Ana had changed her life. If only Ana knew how she'd rescued Patience, taking her from the dark and dirty and bringing her into a place that was bright and clean.

Of course, Ana couldn't know. As far as Patience was concerned, her life started the day she began cleaning house for Anastasia Duchenko. Everything she did beforehand had been washed away.

The hospital doors opened with a soft whoosh, announcing the arrival of another visitor. Immediately, the atmosphere in the room changed, and not because of the June heat disrupting the air-conditioning. The conversations stilled as all attention went to the new arrival. Even the admissions nurse straightened. For a second, Patience wondered if a local celebrity had walked in. The air had that kind of expectancy.

His tailored shirt and silk tie screamed superiority as did his perfect posture. A crown of brown curls kept his features from being too harsh, but only just. No doubt about it, this was a man who expected to be in charge. Bet he wouldn't be kept waiting an hour.

The man strode straight to the admissions window. Patience was about to resume her pacing when she heard him say the name Duchenko.

Couldn't be a coincidence. This could be the break she needed to find out about Ana. She combed her dark hair away from her face, smoothed the front of her tee shirt and stepped forward. "Excuse me, did I hear you ask about Ana Duchenko?"

He turned in her direction. "Who's asking?"

For a moment, Patience lost the ability to speak.

He was looking down at her with eyes the same shade as the blue in a flame, the hue so vivid it couldn't possibly be real. Lit with intensity, they were the kind of eyes that you swore were looking deep inside your soul. "Patience," she replied, recovering. "I'm Patience Rush."

She didn't think it possible for his stare to intensify but it did. "Aunt Anastasia's housekeeper?"

His aunt. Suddenly Patience realized who she was talking to. This was Stuart Duchenko, Ana's great-nephew, the one who called twice a week. Actually, as far as she knew, the only Duchenko relative Ana talked to. Patience didn't know why, other than there'd been some kind of rift and Ana refused to deal with what she called "the rest of the sorry lot." Only Stuart, who managed her financial affairs, remained in her good graces.

"I thought you were in Los Angeles," she said after he introduced himself. Ana said he'd been stuck there for almost a year while some billionaire's family argued over a will.

"My case finished yesterday. What happened?"

"Nigel happened." Nigel being Ana's overly indulged cat.

She could tell from Stuart's expression, he didn't find the answer amusing. Not that she could blame him under the circumstances. She wondered, though, if he would find the story amusing under *any* circumstances. His mouth didn't look like it smiled much.

"He was in the foyer meowing," she continued. "Letting everyone know that his dinner was late. Near as I can guess, when Ana came down the stairs, he started weaving around her ankles, and she lost her balance."

He raised a brow. "Near as you can guess?"

Okay, the man was definitely an attorney; Patience felt she was on trial with all the questions. Of course, that could also be her guilty conscience bothering her. "I was in the dining room polishing the silver. I heard Ana cry out, but by the time I got there, she was already on the floor." She shuddered, remembering. The image of Ana crumpled at the foot of the stairs, moaning, wouldn't leave her soon.

Ana's nephew didn't respond other than to stare long and hard in her direction before turning back to the admissions nurse. "I'd like to see my aunt, please," he said. It might have been said softly, like a request, but there was no mistaking the command in his voice.

The nurse nodded. "I'll see what I can do."

Finally, they were getting somewhere. "I've been trying to get an update on Ana's condition since we arrived, but no one would tell me anything."

"Nor would they," he replied. "Privacy laws. You're not family."

Well, wasn't somebody feeling territorial. Never mind that she was the one who'd brought Ana in and filled out the admissions paperwork. Anyone with two heads could see she cared about the woman. What difference did it make whether she was family or not?

She had to admit, Ana's nephew wasn't at all what she expected. Ana was always talking about how sweet "her Stuart" was. Such a pussycat, she'd coo after hanging up the phone. The man standing next to her wasn't a pussy anything. He was far too predatory. She could practically smell the killer instinct.

Apparently, his singlar request was all they needed, because less than a minute passed before the door to the treatment area opened, and a resident in pale green scrubs stepped out.

"Mr. Duchenko?" He headed toward Stuart, but not, however, before giving Patience a quick once-over. Patience recognized the look. She folded her arms across her chest and pretended she didn't notice. The trick, of course, was to avoid eye contact. Easy to do when the man wasn't looking at your eyes to begin with.

"I'm sorry to keep you waiting," the doctor continued. "We were waiting for the results of your great-aunt's CAT scan."

"How is she?"

"She's got a bimalleolar fracture of her left ankle."

"Bi what?" Patience asked, her stomach tightening a bit. Hopefully the medical jargon sounded more serious than it actually was.

The doctor smiled. "Bimalleolar. Both the bone and her ligaments were injured."

"Meaning what?" Stuart asked the same question she was thinking.

"Meaning she's going to need surgery to stabilize the ankle."

Surgery? Patience felt horrible. She should have been paying closer attention. "Is it risky?"

"At her age, anything involving anesthesia has a risk."

"She's in terrific health," Patience told him, more to reassure herself than anything. "Most people think she's a decade younger."

"That's good. The more active she is, the easier her recovery will be. You know, overall, she's a lucky woman to have only broken her ankle. Falls at her age are extremely dangerous."

"I know," Stuart replied. For some reason he felt the need to punctuate the answer with a look in her direction. "May we see her?"

"She's in exam room six," the doctor replied.

"We'll be taking her upstairs shortly, but you're welcome to sit with her in the meantime."

Exam room six was really a curtained area on the far left-hand side of two rows of curtains. Stuart pulled back the curtain to find Ana tucked under a sheet while a nurse checking the flow of her IV. The soft beep-beep-beep of the machines filled the air. Seeing Ana lying so still with the wires protruding from the sleeve of her gown made Patience sick to her stomach. Normally, the woman was so lively it was easy to forget that she was eighty years old.

"We just administered a painkiller, so she might be a little out of things," the nurse told them. "Don't be alarmed if she sounds confused."

Stuart stepped in first. Patience followed and found him standing by the head of Ana's bed, his long tapered fingers brushing the hair from the elderly woman's face. "Tetya? It's me, Stuart."

The gentle prodding in his voice reminded her of how she would wake her baby sister, Piper, before school. It surprised her. He honestly didn't seem like the gentle type.

Ana's eyelids fluttered open. She blinked, then broke into a drunken smile. "What are you doing here?"

"That fall-alert necklace you refuse to wear notifies me when 911 gets called. I was on my way back from the airport when I got a message."

The smile grew a little wider. "Back? Does that mean you're home for good?"

"It does."

"I missed you, *lapushka*."

"I missed you, too. How are you feeling?"

"Good, now you're here." Her gnarled hand patted his. "Is Nigel okay?"

"Nigel is fine."

"He was a naughty boy. Make sure you tell him I'm disappointed in him."

"I'll let him know." There was indulgence in his voice.

"Don't make him feel too guilty. He didn't mean it." The older woman's eyelids began to droop, sleep taking over once again. "He's stubborn, like you."

"You go ahead and get some sleep, Tetya. I'm back home now. I'll take care of everything."

"Such a good boy. Not at all like your grandfather, thank goodness." She closed her eyes only to open them wide again. "Patience?"

Until then, Patience had lingered at the foot of the bed, not wanting to crowd Ana any more than necessary. Upon hearing her name, she drew closer. "Yes, Ana?"

"There you are," Ana replied. "Thank you."

"You don't have to thank me," she said.

"Yes, I do," the older woman insisted. "You take such good care of me."

Out of the corner of her eyes, she saw Stuart shift his weight and felt the moment his gaze slid in her direction. She kept her attention on Ana and pretended she couldn't see him. "I was only doing what any person would do. Now, why don't you get some rest?"

"Take care of Nigel while I'm here?"

"I will."

"Stuart, too."

She assumed Ana meant for her nephew to help

take care of Nigel. Either that or this was the confusion the nurse mentioned, because the man next to her definitely didn't need taking care of. Certainly not from someone like her.

From the tick in his cheek, Stuart thought the same thing.

They stayed until a different nurse came to check Ana's vitals. The small space was barely big enough for two visitors, let alone three, so Patience stepped outside. To her surprise, Stuart followed.

"You know what's crazy?" she remarked. "That foolish cat causes her to break her ankle and he's still going to get gourmet cat food for dinner." A dinner that, she realized as she did the math in her head, was now several hours late. Hopefully he didn't kick cat litter all over the kitchen floor in retaliation. Or worse, break her ankle.

Stuart was watching her again, his face as dour as before. Apparently drawing the exam room curtain closed off more than Ana's bed. "Are you positive Nigel tripped Ana?" he asked.

That was dumb question. "Of course, I'm sure,"

she replied. "I mean I don't know *for certain*. But, it was dinnertime, and the cat does have this annoying habit of bothering the nearest warm body when he wants to eat. Why are you even asking?" Ana had already told him that the cat had caused the accident.

"Just want to make sure I have all the facts."

Facts? For crying out loud, he sounded as if they were in one of those hour-long detective dramas. "Trust me, you've got all the facts. Nigel is one horrendous pest." Not to mention spoiled rotten. "Besides, who else would trip her? I was the only other person in the house and I..."

He didn't...

She glared up at him through her bangs. "You think I had something to do with Ana's accident?"

"Why would I think that? Ana blames Nigel."

"Because Nigel *tripped* her." His mistrust was serious. Unbelievable.

No, actually, it was very believable. A guy like him, used to the cream of everything. Of course, he'd suspect the help. "Are you suggesting your aunt is lying?"

"Hardly."

"Then why would I be? Lying, that is."

"Did I say you were lying? I told you, I was simply gathering facts. You're the one who read deeper meaning into my questions." Immediately, she opened her mouth to protest, only to have him hold up a finger. "Although," he continued, "you can't blame me if I am suspicious."

Oh, couldn't she? The guy was practically in-sinuating—not practically, he *was* insinuating that she had pushed a helpless little old lady down a flight of stairs. "And why is that?" She folded her arms across her chest. This she had to hear.

"For starters, Aunt Ana hired you directly while I was in Los Angeles."

So that was it. The man was territorial. "In other words, you're upset because Ana didn't talk to you first."

"Yes, I am." Having been expecting a denial, Patience was surprised to hear him agree. "Nor-mally, I vet my family's employees and you, somehow, managed to bypass the process. As a result, I don't know a damn thing about you. For all I know, you could be hiding some deep, dark secret."

Patience's insides chilled. *If only he knew...*

Still, no matter what questionable decisions she'd made in her life, there were lines she'd never dream of crossing. Hurting a defenseless old lady being on top of the list. "You're right," she told him, "you don't know me."

Yanking back the curtain, she returned to Ana's side.

My, my, quite the bundle of moral outrage aren't we? Stuart ignored the twinge from his conscience as he watched Patience sashay behind the curtain. He refused to feel guilty for taking care of his family. After all, until eight months ago, he'd never heard of Patience Rush. Suddenly, the housekeeper was all his aunt could talk about. Patience this, Patience that. *No need to worry about me, Stuart. Patience will take good care of me. Patience is moving into the brownstone.* And the final straw… *Patience takes care of writing out the checks now.*

With Aunt Ana incapacitated, Patience would have an awful lot of power. Or rather, she would have, if he hadn't come home. He kicked himself for not being around the past eleven months. Now his aunt was attached to a stranger he knew nothing about. Ana might be sharp for her age, but when all was said and done, she was still an old woman living alone who had a soft spot for sob stories. Her big heart made her vulnerable to all sorts of exploitation.

It certainly wouldn't be the first time a pretty young thing had tried to grab a piece of the Duchenko fortune.

Unfortunately for Miss Rush, he was no longer a lonely twenty-year-old looking for affection. Nor was he still naive enough to believe people were as guileless as they appeared. Ana was the only family he had left. He'd be damned if he'd let her be burned the way he had been.

There was the rustle of a curtain, and Ana's gurney appeared on its way toward the elevator.

As she passed by, the older woman gave him a sleepy wave. Stuart grabbed her hand and pressed the wizened knuckles to his lips. "See you soon, Tetya," he whispered.

"The surgical waiting area is on the third floor," the nurse told him. "If you want to stay there, we can let you know as soon as they're finished."

"Thank you."

Patience's soft voice answered before he had the chance. Immediately, his mouth drew into a tight line. "You're planning to wait, too?"

"Of course. I'm not going to be able to sleep until I know you're okay," she told Ana.

Ana smiled. "But Nigel…"

"Nigel will be fine," he said. While he wasn't crazy about Miss Rush hanging around, he wasn't about to start an argument over his aunt's hospital gurney. "Don't you worry."

"Besides, it'll do him good to wait," Patience added, "seeing as how this whole accident is his fault." She raised her eyes, daring him to say otherwise. "I promise, I'll go home and feed him as soon as you're out of surgery."

The sedatives were starting to kick in. Ana's smile was weak and sloppy. "Such a good girl," she murmured before closing her eyes.

Oh, yeah, a real sweetheart, he thought to himself. The way she so casually referred to the brownstone as home rankled him to no end. It was like ten years ago all over again, only this time, instead of a beguiling blonde worming her way into their lives, it was a brunette with hooded eyes and curves that wouldn't quit.

Interesting that she chose to downplay her sexuality. A tactical decision, perhaps? If so, it didn't work. A burlap sack couldn't mute those assets. Even he had to admit to a stir of appreciation the first time he saw her.

She was hiding more than her figure, too. Don't think he didn't notice how she looked away when he mentioned having secrets. There was a lot more to Patience Rush than met the eye. And he intended to find out what.

They spent the time Anna was in surgery on opposite sides of the waiting area, Stuart moving chairs together to create a makeshift work area while Patience made do with out-of-date women's magazines. Having read up on last fall's fashions and learned how to spot if her spouse was having an online affair, she was left with nothing to do but lean back in her chair and shoot daggers at Ana's nephew.

Who did he think he was, suggesting she had something to do with Ana's fall? Like she could ever. Anastasia Duchenko saved her life with this job. Every morning, she woke up grateful for the opportunity. To be able to walk down the street with her head held high. To not have to scrub herself raw to feel clean. Finally, she had a job she could be proud of. Be a *person* she could be proud of.

Even if the whole situation was built on a lie, she thought, guilt washing over her the way it always did.

She wasn't proud of her behavior—add it to a long list of regrets—but she made amends every single day by working hard and taking care of Ana. You wouldn't find a better housekeeper and companion on Beacon Hill. She would never—ever—jeopardize the gift Ana had given her.

Tell Stuart Duchenko that, though. If he learned she'd lied her way into the job, he'd kick her to the curb before she could say *but*... And who knows what he'd do if he learned what she used to do for a living before finding Ana? She shuddered to think.

The sound of rustling papers caught her attention. Looking over, she saw Stuart pinching the bridge of his nose. The man looked worn-out. Patience had to admit, for all his jerkiness, he appeared genuinely concerned for his great-aunt. The adoration Ana talked about seemed to run both ways.

"Mr. Duchenko?" A small African-American nurse in a bright pink smock rounded the corner, bringing them both to their feet. "Dr. Richardson just called. He'll be down shortly to talk with you, but he wanted you to know that your aunt came through the surgery without problem and is on her way to recovery."

"Oh, thank goodness." The words rushed from

Patience's mouth, drawing Stuart's attention. Their eyes met, and she saw agreement in their blue depths. In this, they were on the same page.

"Can we see her?" he asked.

"She'll be in recovery for several hours, I'm afraid," the nurse replied with a shake of her head. "In fact, considering the hour, they might not move her until morning. You're better off getting some sleep and coming back tomorrow."

Patience watched as a protest worked its way across the man's features. She had a feeling if he insisted, he'd get his way. Better judgment must have stepped in—either that or fatigue— because he nodded. "How long before Dr. Richardson gets here?"

"He said he was on his way down, so I don't think it'll be more than five or ten minutes."

It turned out to be closer to twenty. When he did arrive, Dr. Richardson gave a succinct report, without a whole lot of new information. They'd inserted a plate and some screws to stabilize the break. Ana came through the surgery without issue. They'd monitor her throughout the night for complications. No, he wasn't sure how long she'd need to stay in the hospital.

Still, Patience left the waiting room feeling that Ana was in good hands. Another plus: Stuart was on the phone so she was spared any more accusations. From here on in, she'd do her best to avoid the man.

A pair of angry green eyes greeted her when she unlocked the door to Ana's brownstone. Patience wasn't intimidated. "Don't give me attitude, mister. This whole night is your fault."

With what Patience swore was a huff, Nigel jumped down from the entryway table and ran toward the kitchen. An urgent wail traveled back to her ears a second later. "Puleeze," she called, "like you were ever in danger of starving."

Arms hugging her body, Patience made her way along the corridor, thinking the slap of her sandals against her feet sounded abnormally loud. It felt weird being in the brownstone alone. While Ana went out a lot, the woman was seldom gone past eight o'clock and so her absence hung thick in the emptiness. A gleam caught Patience's eye as she passed the dining room. The silver set she'd been polishing when Ana fell still sat on the table, the cloth on the floor where she'd dropped it upon hearing Ana's cry. The moment replayed as she curled her fingers around the soft material, the image of her savior crumpled at the base of the stairs making her nauseous. Thank goodness, Ana was going to be all right. Tomorrow she would work on making the house perfect for her return. Starting with making sure the tea set gleamed.

Nigel had resumed his meowing. Patience tossed the cloth on the table. "Oh, for goodness' sake, I'm coming. Five minutes will not kill you."

She turned around only to walk into a tall, muscular wall. "What the—" Why hadn't she brought the teapot along with her as a weapon?

Stuart Duchenko arched a dark eyebrow. Even in the partially lit hallway, his eyes shone bright. "Did I startle you?"

He knew perfectly well he had. "How did you get in?"

"Same way you did. With my key." He held up

a key ring. "Or did you think you were the only one Ana gave access to?"

"Don't be silly. I didn't hear the doorbell is all." They were way too close. Close enough she could smell the breath mint he'd obviously just finished. She wasn't used to sweet-smelling breath, not from men anyway. It caught her off guard, which had to be the reason she didn't step back at first contact. She stepped back now, and spied a pair of suitcases at the base of the stairs.

Seeing where her gaze had gone, he gave a shrug. "I sold my condominium before leaving for LA. Until I find a new place, this is more convenient than a hotel."

Convenient for what? Keeping an eye on her?

It was as if he read her thoughts. "Ana made the suggestion back when I first left. Of course, I'm sure she wasn't expecting to be in the hospital at the time. My being here won't be a problem for you, will it?" he asked. The gleam in his eye dared her to say that it was.

Patience would be damned if she'd give him

the satisfaction. "Of course not. Why would your staying here be a problem for me?"

"Extra work for you. I know you're used to it being only you and Aunt Ana."

Another veiled comment. The man was full of them, wasn't he? "Extra work won't be a problem. Cleaning is cleaning. Besides, like you said, it's temporary, right?"

"We can only hope. I figure I'll stay until Ana gets back on her feet. Make sure there aren't any problems."

What kind of problems? Was he afraid Patience would take off with the silver? Why didn't he just come out and say what was really on his mind?

"You don't trust me, do you?"

"No, I don't."

Finally, the truth was out in the open. She appreciated the bluntness. Beat phony friendliness any day. Didn't mean she wasn't going to set him straight though.

"Your aunt trusts me. Are you saying Ana isn't a good judge of character?"

She stepped back into his personal space, making sure to maintain eye contact and letting him know his answer didn't intimidate her one bit. The posture brought her close enough that she could smell his skin. Like his breath, his body smelled clean and fresh, despite having been traveling all day. An antsy, fluttering sensation started in the pit of her stomach. Butterflies, but with a nervous edge. The notion that she was out of her league passed briefly through her mind.

Stuart's eyes stayed locked with hers. A Mexican standoff, with each of them waiting for the other to blink. "My aunt has a generous heart. I, on the other hand…"

"Let me guess. You don't."

Patience sensed rather than saw his smile. "I prefer to lead with my head. Less chance for mistakes."

"Except, in this case, you're already mistaken."

"We'll find out, won't we?" he said. "Since I'll be living here, we'll have plenty of time to get acquainted. Who knows what secrets we'll learn about each other?"

Patience managed to wait until he disappeared

upstairs before hissing. What was it with him and secrets?

You didn't exactly help your cause, did you? Challenging him like that. A smart person would have let his comments pass, refused to give him the satisfaction of a reaction. But, *nooo*, she had to call him out. Might as well hold a sign over her head reading I've Got a Secret!

So much for leaving her past behind. She should have known that a future built on a lie—even an innocent one—wouldn't last. Ana was going to be so disappointed in her.

She bit her knuckle, forcing down her panic. No need to start packing just yet. This bluster was probably nothing more than a scare tactic to put her in her place. To make up for not having a say in hiring her, no doubt. A few days from now, after seeing how well Patience did her job, he'd back off and leave her alone.

It could happen, right?

CHAPTER TWO

THERE WAS A weight vibrating on his chest. He must have left the door open when he came upstairs. "It better be light out, Nigel," he muttered. Freeing a hand from under the covers, he felt around until his fingers found fur. Immediately, the purring increased as Nigel leaned into the touch. A sad voice in his head noted this was the most action he'd had in his bed in way too long. "Hey, be careful with the claws, buddy," he said when the cat began kneading the blanket. "I might need those parts someday." You never knew. A social life might spontaneously develop. Stranger things had happened.

At work, people considered him a workaholic, but the truth was, he'd never been what people would call popular. He discovered early that being a Duchenko heir meant being judged and misunderstood. As a kid, his awkwardness was labeled snobbery. As he got older, his social desirability was measured in terms of his bank account. He had to be constantly on guard, assessing the motives of every person that crossed his path. The one time he hadn't...well, that had taught him two more lessons: Don't let sex cloud your judgment and even family members will screw you over. Except for Ana, that is. Ana was the one family member who loved him for him.

Nigel's head butted his hand, a not so subtle way of saying *more petting, less thinking.* Giving a half sigh, Stuart opened his eyes, then blinked when he saw Nigel in perfect focus. He'd forgotten to take out his contact lenses again. No wonder his eyes felt as if they had sand in them. What time was it anyway? Yesterday had wiped him out so badly he barely remembered falling into bed.

Not too wiped out to go toe-to-toe with the housekeeper, though. It was a bit arrogant of him showing up without warning, but he'd wanted to catch her off guard. To see how she'd react to learning she wouldn't have the run of the brownstone.

Turned out she reacted to the blind side better than most of his legal opponents.

Most of his legal opponents didn't have eyes that lit up like chocolate diamonds, either. Dark and sinfully rich, their spark got his adrenaline going in a way practicing law sure didn't. A guy could make a career out of looking for ways to make those eyes light up.

What was that about not letting sex cloud his judgment? Ignoring Nigel's protest, he rolled onto his side and reached for the phone on the nightstand. It was early, he thought, noting the time, but not so early to reach an associate. The ambitious ones practically slept at the firm. A few minutes of scrolling through his contacts found him the name he wanted.

Just as he expected, Bob Cunningham answered on the first ring. "Welcome back. I hear congratulations are in order." He was referring to the LA case.

"Too bad the former Mrs. Wentworth didn't

come to her senses last year." Instead, she'd put her late husband's family through hell and sentenced Stuart to months of aggravation, not to mention opening the door for Patience Rush. "There are a couple details to iron out that I'll talk to you about later. In the meantime, I need some background research done. A woman named Patience Rush."

"Is that her real name?"

Good question. Strangely enough, he hoped the quirky moniker was real. "That's for you to tell me." He gave him what details he knew.

"You're not giving the investigator much to work with," Bob replied.

"He's worked with less."

"True. What client number should I bill?"

"SD100." On the other end of the line, there was a soft intake of breath. Stuart seldom used his discretionary fund, but the firm's investigator was the best around. He'd reimburse the firm later.

"Um…"

"What?" Stuart asked.

The associate paused. "This might take a while. We've tapped him for a couple other projects."

And clients always came before personal. Stuart understood. "Just tell him to get to it as soon as he can."

In the meantime, he'd just have to keep a close eye on Patience Rush. Thinking about her eyes, he couldn't help but smile. There were worse jobs in the world.

A short while later, having showered and changed, he headed downstairs only to hear muffled voices coming from the kitchen. One muffled voice actually. He found Patience crouched over Nigel's food dish, brandishing a dustpan and broom. "You'd think a cat who acts like he's starving wouldn't drop pieces of food all over the place," she muttered. "One of these days, I'm going to toss the whole bowl out. Let's see what you do then."

A chuckle rose in his throat. Nigel had a way of making all of them talk as if he understood. He leaned a shoulder against the door frame. "Not a cat person, I take it."

She gasped before looking up at him with a glare. "Do you always sneak up on people?"

There they were again, those chocolate-diamond eyes. He crossed his legs to keep his jeans from growing tight. "I didn't know walking around the house was considered sneaking."

"Then you should walk louder," she replied. "Or wear shoes."

He looked down at his bare feet. "I'll keep that in mind. May I ask what the cat did to earn your wrath?"

"Nigel isn't a cat. He's a four-legged spoiled brat."

As had been all of Ana's cats. His aunt tended to overindulge the strays she adopted. Pushing herself to her feet, Patience swayed her way across the room to the trash can. Stuart found himself wondering if the seductive gait was natural or on purpose. "Sounds like the two of you have a great relationship," he remarked.

"Mine and Nigel's relationship is just fine.

Why?" She took her foot off the receptacle latch, causing the lid to close with a loud slap. "Afraid I'll try to push him down the stairs, too?"

"Nah. A woman as smart as you would know hurting Nigel is the quickest way to getting on Ana's bad side."

She gave him a long look. "Was that supposed to be a compliment?"

In a way, yes. He did think she was smart. "If you want to take it as such."

"Gosh, thanks. I'll try not to let it go to my head."

Smart and quick-witted. She was dressed similarly to yesterday in jeans, a T-shirt and a cardigan sweater, her hair pulled back with one of those plastic hair bands. For the first time he looked closely at her features. Yesterday, he'd been too distracted by her eyes, but today he noticed more intricate details like the long slope of her nose and the way her teeth met her lower lip in a slight overbite. A two-inch scar cut across her right cheekbone. Time had caused it to fade. In fact, with makeup, it'd be barely noticeable, but since she was again bare faced, he could see the jagged edges of a cut that should have had stitches. The scar bothered him, like seeing a crack on the surface of a crystal vase. It didn't belong.

Patience cleared her throat. Realizing he'd been staring, he covered his action by adjusting his glasses. This might be one of those rare moments when he was grateful for them. He detested wearing the heavy black frames. The look might be considered stylish now, but it simply reminded him of his younger, awkward days. Then again, maybe a reminder was a good thing, given the awareness swirling around his insides this morning.

He reached for a change of topic. "Do I smell coffee?" There was a distinct aroma of French roast in the air, a unique scent in his tea-drinking aunt's home.

Patience nodded her head toward a stainless steel coffeemaker tucked in the faraway corner. "Cream and sugar are in the dining room. Do you prefer a full breakfast or continental."

"Neither." Was she offering to make him breakfast? Considering the circumstances, he wasn't sure if he should be flattered or suspicious. "Are you waiting on me?" he asked when she took a coffee mug from the cupboard. "Why?"

"Because it's my job," she replied. "I serve breakfast every morning. So long as someone's here, I'll keep on serving it." Filling the cup, she handed it to him.

Stuart stared into the black liquid. What gives? Last night, Patience had made it quite clear that she didn't appreciate his staying at the brownstone, yet here she was pouring him coffee and offering breakfast. Citing her job. Was she truly that dedicated or was this some kind of tactic to throw him off his game? If the latter, it was working.

"Something wrong?" she asked. "Would you feel better if I drank the cup first?"

"All right, you've made your point," he said, setting the coffee cup down. "You didn't appreciate my questioning Ana's accident."

"Not the accident—me. You all but accused me of pushing your aunt down the stairs."

Yes, he had. Now that he thought about it, the accusation wasn't his finest moment. Treating the woman like a hostile witness wouldn't accomplish anything. A situation like this called for a more delicate touch. "I'm sorry," he said. "I tend to be wary when it comes to strangers around my family."

"Well, I tend to have a problem with being accused of crimes I didn't commit," she replied, snapping his olive branch in two. "Now if you'll excuse me, I've got a job to do."

"Can you believe the guy? I think he actually considered that comment an apology."

"Some people aren't very good with apologies." Her sister Piper's face filled the screen of her smartphone. Thank goodness for Wi-Fi and internet chat apps. She so needed a friendly ear right now and Piper was the one person in this world she could trust. Patience called her as soon as she sat down at Ana's desk.

"Maybe he's one of those people," her sister continued.

"Probably because in his mind he's never wrong." She sighed. "I can't believe I'm going to be stuck working for the man while Ana's in the hospital. Talk about a nightmare."

"Oh, come on, it won't be that bad."

"Are you kidding? We're living under the same roof. How am I supposed to avoid him?"

"I doubt he's going to be hanging around the house."

Wanna bet? Patience caught the smirk in his eyes last night. He probably considered the arrangement the perfect opportunity to vet her. Who used words like *vet* anyway? Couldn't he say *check her out* like a normal person.

"I don't like him," she said. "He's…"

"He's what?"

Too imposing. With his unwavering blue eyes and long lean torso. "There's something about the way he looks at me," she said, keeping her thoughts to herself.

"Guys are always looking at you."

"Not like this." Those guys were skeevy. All hands and leers. "It's like he's trying to read my mind." She wasn't used to a man looking at her as anything more than a chick with a nice rack. It was unnerving to have a man look deeper. "Plus, he keeps talking about secrets. I'm worried one of these times I'll slip up and say something incriminating."

"So, don't talk to him. There's no rule that says a housekeeper has to be chatty."

"True." Except she seemed unable to help herself.

"If it helps," Piper added, "I watched a movie the other night where the woman drugged her husband's dinner so he'd leave her alone. You could always try that."

"Oh, sure." It was exactly the laugh she needed. "Because my life isn't enough like a made-for-television movie. Seriously, though, what am I going to do?"

"You could try telling the truth."

Patience shook her head. "I can't."

"Why not? I bet Ana won't care, especially

once she hears the whole story. I mean, it's not like you had other choices. Surely, Ana would understand that you did what you had to do."

Maybe, but what about the reason Patience stayed for as long as she did? There were some secrets Piper didn't know and was better off never knowing. That particular shame was Patience's and Patience's alone.

Again, she shook her head. "I'll just have to stay on my toes is all. Hopefully, when Ana starts to feel better, he'll lose interest. A rich, handsome lawyer? I'm sure he's got better things to focus on than the hired help."

"You didn't mention he was handsome," Piper said, giving her a smirk.

"He's…good-looking," Patience replied rolling her eyes. *Handsome* wasn't the right word. "Not that it makes a difference. I'm more concerned about keeping my job."

"You're going to be fine, You're one of the most resilient people I know."

Patience wished she shared her sister's confidence. "Let's talk about something else," she said. She was tired of whining. "How's school?"

"Um…good. French pastries are turning out to be a challenge."

"Bet yours taste fantastic. Any way you can mail me your homework?" She was so proud of Piper. Winning a scholarship to study cooking in Paris. Piper's success made everything worthwhile. "And how's work?" Her sister was earning room and board as a live-in maid. "Your boss must be psyched to have a gourmet cook on staff."

"Frederic doesn't eat home much."

The grainy camera image failed to mask the shadow that crossed Piper's face, immediately sending Patience's maternal instincts into high alert. "What's wrong?" she asked.

"Nothing," Piper replied quickly. "I'm just bummed not to have someone to cook for is all. I miss you."

Homesickness. Of course. Patience should have realized. This was the longest the two of them had ever been apart. Hard as it was on her, it had to be doubly hard on Piper, alone in a foreign country. "I miss you too Pipe. But, hey, we've got Wi-Fi. You can call me anytime you want."

Piper smiled. "Back at you." Offscreen, a noise occurred, causing her sister to look over her shoulder. "Hey, I've got to go," she said. "The boss just walked in. Don't let Ana's nephew intimidate you, okay? You're just as good as he is."

"Thanks. I love you."

"Love you, too."

Patience's smile faded as soon as she clicked off. Piper had such faith in her. It wasn't that she was completely ashamed of everything she'd done in life, she thought, setting the phone aside. Raising Piper, for instance. She couldn't be prouder of the woman her baby sister had become. Giving Piper a chance for a real future had always been what mattered the most. Her baby sister would never have to degrade herself to pay the bills.

A knock sounded behind her, making her start. "You can't accuse me of sneaking up on you this time," Stuart said. "I knocked."

Yes, he had, and he now stood in the doorway

with his arms folded like a long, lean statue. It wasn't surprising that he managed to look as regally imposing in jeans and bare feet as he did in a suit. Patience had a feeling he could wear a bunch of rags and still look wealthy. Even the glasses that, on someone else would look geeky, looked more geek-chic on him. Actually, much as she hated to admit it, the frames looked adorable on him.

Some of her bangs had slipped free of her hair band. She brushed them aside to disguise her reaction. "Do you need something?" she asked.

"It dawned on me that I sounded—are you writing out checks?"

His gaze had dropped to the ledger that lay open on the desk. What now?

"I'm reconciling the checkbook. Ana likes a paper record in addition to the online version." She considered adding that his aunt had asked her to take over the task because her math was getting a bit fuzzy, but that would only make her sound more defensive than she did, and she refused to feel guilty for doing her job.

"I never did understand her insistence on two records," He replied. She'd expected a far more snide comment. Walking over to the desk, he studied the laptop screen from over her shoulder. "Seems like way too much opportunity for mistakes."

"I've tried to tell Ana the same thing." As much as she tried not to be, Patience found herself acutely aware of his chest hovering behind her ear. The scent of his body wash lingered in the air. Clean. Crisp. She couldn't help herself; she inhaled deeply.

"You forgot to record check number 3521," he said, pointing at the screen.

Sure enough, there was an unrecorded check. "This is the biggest problem," she said. "Ana always forgets to mark the checks in both places."

"I thought you wrote the checks?"

"I write out the monthly checks for the bills. That doesn't mean your aunt doesn't write out her own ocassionally. Especially when she want to give money to the humane society. See?" She pointed to the written ledger. "Check 3521 in her handwriting."

She shifted in her hair, so she could better confront him. "Are you going to question everything I do while you're living here? Because if so, it's going to make for a very long stay."

"I wasn't questioning anything. All I did was point out you missed a check."

Right. And his pointing out had nothing to do with his distrust. "Look," she said, "I know you don't like me—"

"I never said I didn't like you."

Patience blinked. "You didn't?"

"No. I said I didn't trust you. There's a difference."

Not much. "Gee, thanks. I feel so much better."

A hint of color found its way to his cheeks. It, along with his quick, sheepish smile, dulled her annoyance. "I'm not saying this right at all," he said. "I came in because I realized what I said back in the kitchen didn't come out as apologetically as it should have. What I should have said was that I'm sorry for treating you like a trial witness last night. I should have let the matter drop after Ana corroborated your story."

"Actually," Patience replied, "what you should have said was that you're sorry for even suggesting I'd hurt your aunt."

Stuart grabbed the edge of the desk, trapping her between his two arms. Body wash and heat buffeted the space between them, the combination making Patience's pulse quicken. She looked up to meet a gaze that was bright and resolute. "Ana is the only family I have," he said. "I won't apologize for trying to protect her."

This was where Patience should retaliate with angry defiance. Unfortunately, she understood where Stuart was coming from. When it came to keeping your family safe, you did whatever you had to do. No matter what.

Still, she wasn't ready to let him off the hook. "Let's get something straight," she said, straightening her spine. "I like Ana. She's been good to me. Real good. I would never hurt her. I don't care how good your reason is—you are a jerk for thinking otherwise."

They were back to Mexican standoff territory, with their eyes challenging one another. Patience focused on keeping her breath even. She didn't know if it was his scent, his close proximity, or the thrill of having held her ground, but she could feel the adrenaline surging through her. When Stuart broke the moment with a slow, lazy smile, her heart jumped. The thrill of victory, she decided.

"Yes, I was," he said. "A jerk, that is."

"Finally, we agree with something." She sat back, only to realize the new posture placed her in the crook of his arm. Instinct screamed for her to straighten up again, but that would imply she was nervous, and since she wasn't nervous she forced herself to look relaxed. "Apology accepted."

Stuart responded with a low chuckle before— thankfully—shifting positions and releasing her. Patience was surprised how much she missed his scent when it disappeared.

"How about we start over with a clean slate?" he said. "Hi. I'm Stuart Duchenko."

She stared at his extended hand. For some reason, the gesture kicked off warning bells. "Why?" she asked.

"Why what?"

"Why the one-eighty?" A dozen hours ago, he was smirking with suspicion. Now he wanted to be friends?

He'd obviously expected the question, because he chuckled again. "Because you're right, I was being a jerk. And, because Ana would have my head if she saw the way I was acting. Our bickering like a couple of twelve-year-olds won't help her. Therefore, I'm hoping we can be civil for her sake."

He had a point. Ana would expect better of her, as well. "Does this mean you've decided to trust me?"

"Let's not go crazy. I am, however, willing to give you the chance to prove me wrong."

"Well, isn't that mighty big of you." Although, in truth, they had something in common. She didn't trust him, either.

His hand was still extended, waiting for her acceptance. Fine. She could be the bigger person, too. For Ana's sake.

"I'm Patience Rush," she said, wrapping her fingers around his palm.

His grip was firm and confident, more so than she expected. Patience was shocked at the power traveling up her arm.

You're playing with fire, a tiny voice whispered in her ear. Stuart wasn't some sour-smelling creep she could hold off with an expressionless stare. He was a man whose clout and influence could ruin her life. But, like a shining red sign blinking "Do Not Touch," she couldn't resist the challenge.

"Nice to meet you, Patience. I look forward to getting to know you."

"Same here."

She wasn't sure what to say next and, based on the awkward silence, neither did he. The strangest energy had begun humming around them. Wrapping them together, as if the two of them were suddenly on the same page. Weird. Other than Piper, Patience had always made it a rule to keep an invisible wall between herself and the rest of the world. To feel a connection of any kind left her off balance.

Stuart's smile mirrored her insides. Tentative and crooked. "Look at us being all civil."

"Let's not go crazy," she replied, quoting him. "It's only been a minute. Let's see how we do at the end of the day."

"I'm up for the challenge if you are."

Oh, she was more than up for it. If being civil led to him dropping all his talk of "secrets," then she'd civil him to death.

CHAPTER THREE

To her complete and utter amazement, he didn't insist on supervising her work. Instead, he left her with a friendly "Don't forget to mark down check 3521." Probably planning to double-check her work later, Patience decided. She took more care than usual to make sure the ledgers were perfect.

After lunch, Stuart went to the hospital to spend time with Ana while she stayed behind to wage war with the brownstone windows. She thought about visiting as well, but decided to wait until evening so Stuart would see how seriously she took her job.

And, okay, maybe part of her wanted to avoid him. Being civil would be a lot easier if they didn't see each other. The energy shift when they shook hands still had her thrown. Ever since, there'd been this inexplicable fluttering in her stomach that no amount of window cleaning could shake. A reminder that she wasn't dealing with an ordinary man, but rather someone a class above the creeps and losers who'd crossed her path over the years. Talk about two different worlds, she thought with an unbidden shiver. All the more reason to avoid him as much as possible.

And so, armed with cleaner and crumpled newspaper, she polished glass until the smell of vinegar clung to her nostrils and there wasn't a streak to be found. As she stretched out the small of her back, she checked the clock on the parlor mantel. Five o'clock. Time to feed the beast. She was surprised Nigel wasn't upstairs with her, meowing up a storm. He wasn't in the hallway, either.

"You better not be hiding somewhere thinking about pouncing on me," she called out as she trotted down the stairs. "I can tell you right now scaring me won't get you on my good side."

"I'll keep that in mind," Stuart replied. He

looked impossibly at home, standing at the counter with a cat food can in his hand and Nigel weaving in and around his legs.

"What are you doing here?" she asked, only to realize how abrupt she sounded. They were supposed to be acting civil after all. "I mean, I thought you were visiting Ana." That sounded much nicer.

"I got home a few minutes ago and Nigel met me at the door. Nearly broke my ankle demanding supper."

"No way!" She purposely exaggerated her disbelief. "Good thing you weren't on the stairs." Her smirk couldn't have faded even if she wanted it to. *Go Nigel.* Kitty earned himself extra tuna.

To his credit, Stuart had the decency to look apologetic. "Point made. I was wrong."

"Told you so." Since they were being civil, she kept the rest of her gloating to herself. Instead, she bent down to retrieve Nigel's bowl, making sure she gave the cat an extra scratch under the chin when he ran over to see her. "How is Ana?" she asked.

His expression changed in a flash, growing somber. "They've got her on pain medicine so she mostly sleeps, and the couple times she did wake up, she was confused. The nurses told me that's pretty common, especially at her age." He breathed hard through his nostrils. A nonverbal *but*...

Patience felt herself softening toward the man even more. Seeing Ana so weak had upset her, too, and she had been around to see how active Ana had been. Goodness only knows how shocked Stuart must have felt having missed the last eight months. "I'm sure she'll be back to her feisty self in no time," she said, trying to reassure him. And herself, too, maybe.

"That's what the nurses said."

"But...?" There was a hesitancy in his response that once again left the word hanging in the air.

"Did you know one-fourth of senior citizens who break a hip die within six months?"

"Not Ana." No way was he going down that road. "She'd kill you if she heard you. Besides, she broke an ankle, not a hip, so your statistic doesn't apply."

"You're right. It doesn't." A smile graced his features. Forced maybe, but it erased the sadness from his face. Patience was glad. He looked much better with his dimples showing. Not that he didn't look good when serious, but his appeal definitely increased when his eyes sparkled.

"And Ana would kill me," he added, and they shared another smile before Stuart looked away to finish feeding Nigel. Patience waited until he'd scraped the sides of the cat food can before placing the bowl back in its place. "I was planning to visit Ana tonight," she told him.

"Me too. Right after dinner."

Shoot! She'd completely forgotten about dinner. Normally, by this point in the day, she'd have started cooking, but she'd been so engrossed in cleaning the windows—and trying not to think about Stuart—that everything else slipped her mind. "I…um…" Combing the bangs from her eyes, she caught a whiff of vinegar and winced at the odor. "I hope you don't mind simple. I forgot to get the meat out to thaw."

"Don't worry about it. I'll grab something on the way. I've been dying for an Al's Roast Beef."

"No way."

"What, you don't like Al's?"

"No, I love it." She was surprised he did. Al's was a little hole-in-the-wall near the subway overpass. The kind of place you weren't one-hundred-percent sure passed the health inspection, although it did have the most amazing burgers and roast beef sandwiches. She would have pegged Stuart as preferring something more upscale and elegant, like the wine bar up the street. "Can't beat their barbecue special."

"Would you like to join me?"

Join him? The hair on the back of her neck started to rise, much the way it did when he'd suggested they start over. She didn't trust this warmer, gentler Stuart. Especially since he said he still didn't trust her.

What was he up to?

"We both need to eat," he replied, picking up

on her hesitation. "We're both going to the hospital. Why not go together?"

Why not? She could give a bunch of reasons, starting with the fact she should be avoiding him, not giving him an opportunity to dig for information.

"Plus, I owe you an apology for being wrong about Nigel."

"You do owe me that," Patience replied.

"So, is that a yes?" His expectant smile was so charming it caused her stomach to do a tiny somersault. As sure a sign as any that she should say no. Playing with fire, the voice in her head reminded her.

Except that smile was too darn hard to refuse. "Sure," she replied. "Why not?"

She regretted her response as soon as they arrived at Al's. Actually, she regretted it as soon as the words left her mouth and Stuart flashed a knee-buckling smile, but arriving at the restaurant sealed the deal—*restaurant* being a loose description. Beacon Hill types considered the banged-up booths and ketchup stains "atmosphere." Patience considered it dirty. The place reminded her too much of the old days.

"We could do takeout if you'd rather," Stuart said, correctly interpreting her expression. "Go eat by the river."

Patience shook her head. "No. Here will be fine." A picnic by the river sounded too nice, and, frankly, the situation was strange enough without the atmosphere feeling like a date.

This kinder, gentler Stuart made her nervous. They weren't friends—not by a long shot—and she wasn't really sure she bought his apology excuse. So why were they out to dinner together?

After placing their orders, they took seats in a booth toward the rear of the restaurant. One of the cleaner tables, if that was saying anything. Immediately, Patience took out a package of hand wipes and began cleaning the crumbs from the surface, earning a chuckle from Stuart.

"You do realize you're off the clock, right?" he asked.

"You want to eat on a dirty table?" she shot

back. She was beginning to dislike his laugh. Rich and thick, the sound slipped down her spine like warm chocolate syrup, making her insides quiver every time she heard it. Doubling down on her cleaning efforts, she did her best to wash both the crumbs and the sensation away. "I don't even want to think about what the kitchen looks like," she continued.

There was a splash of dried cola near the napkin dispenser. She went at it with vigor. "Piper would have a nutty if she saw this place."

"Who's Piper?"

Drat. She didn't realize she'd spoken aloud. This really was a mistake. Not five minutes in and she'd opened the door to personal questions. Fortunately, Piper was the one personal subject she could talk about forever. "She's my sister."

"Let me guess, she's into cleaning, too?"

"No, cooking." Her chest grew full. "She's studying to be a chef. In Paris." She made a point of emphasizing the location.

"Is that so?"

Based on the spark in Stuart's eye, Patience decided it was admiration and not disbelief coloring his voice, and her pride expanded some more. "She was accepted last fall. It's always been her dream to become a famous chef."

"You must be proud."

"Proud doesn't begin to cover it. I think she's going to be the next Top Chef, she's that talented. Ever since she was a kid, she had a knack for taking ingredients you'd never thought would go together and turning them into something delicious. Once, I came home and found her making jalapeño pancakes."

"Were they any good?"

"Believe it or not, they were. Alhough she got flour everywhere. Took me all night to clean the film from the countertop." A waste of time since the roaches came scrounging anyway. The thought only made her smile fade a little. As always, her pride in Piper's talent overruled the bad.

Their conversation was interrupted by a group of college students settling into the booth behind them. Their laughter barely disguised the popping of beer cans.

"I forgot this place was BYOB," Stuart remarked. "We could have brought a bottle of Merlot to go with our meal."

"I'm not sure this is a Merlot kind of place," Patience replied.

"Good point. Beer then."

She tried and failed to stop her grimace.

"You don't like beer?"

"I don't like the smell." He wouldn't either if he'd spent years breathing sour, stale air.

Stuart was clearly curious, but thankfully he didn't push. At least not right then. Instead, he stretched his arms along the back of the booth, the position pulling his shirt taut across his torso and emphasizing the contours beneath the cotton. Patience wondered if he realized he was the most superior-looking man in the place.

"So, your sister's dream is to become a famous chef," he said. "What's yours?"

To make sure Piper's dream came true. Patience busied herself with pulling napkins from the dispenser. "I don't know what you mean."

"Oh, come on. Surely you didn't always want to be a housekeeper?"

He was fishing. Looking for clues about this so-called agenda he thought she had regarding his aunt. What would he think if she told him her childhood hadn't allowed for dreams or aspirations? Or that there was a time when even being a housekeeper seemed out of her reach? Would he trust her more or less? Patience could guess the answer.

"I thought we called a truce," she said, dodging the question.

"Hey, I was just making conversation. I didn't realize I'd asked you to reveal a state secret."

He had a point. Maybe she was overreacting just a little. It certainly wasn't his fault he'd stumbled too close to a bad topic. "Teacher," she said softly. "When I was little, I wanted to be a teacher."

"There now, that wasn't so hard, was it?" Damn

him for having a charming smile as he spoke. "What changed your mind?"

"I grew up," she replied. The words came out sharper than she intended, causing a stunned expression. "And my mother died, leaving me to raise Piper." She was probably telling him way too much, but she figured revealing some facts was smarter than acting prickly. "Hard to go to school and raise your kid sister." Not that there was money for school to begin with, but he didn't need to know that.

"I'm sorry. How old were you?"

"Eighteen."

"That must have been tough."

"We managed. How about you?" She rushed to change the subject before he could ask anything further. "Did you always want to be a lawyer?"

He laughed again. "Of course not. No little boy wants to be lawyer. I wanted to be a professional baseball player."

"What happened?"

"I grew up," he said, repeating her answer. In his case, instead of sounding prickly, the words came out sad, despite his clearly trying to sound otherwise. "Turns out you have to have athletic ability to be a professional athlete—or a child athlete, for that matter."

Looking at him, she found his protest a bit hard to believe. "You look pretty athletic to me," she said. His arched brow made her blush. "I mean, I'm sure you weren't as bad as you make it sound."

"I had bad eyes, allergies and childhood asthma. Trust me, no one was ever going to confuse me with Babe Ruth. Or John Ruth for that matter."

"Who's John Ruth?"

"Exactly." He grinned, and she got the joke. He was worse than a guy who didn't exist.

"So," he continued, "with the Hall of Fame out of the picture, I found myself steered toward the family business."

"I thought your family business was mining?" Ana was always talking about Duchenko silver.

"Not since the turn of the century. Grandpa Theodore turned it into law. Thankfully. Can you see me coughing and squinting my way through a silver mine?"

No, she thought with a laugh. He definitely belonged to suits and luxury surroundings. His choice of words did make her curious, however. "You said steered. You didn't choose?"

"Sometimes you find yourself on a path without realizing it," he replied with a shrug.

Patience could sure relate to that, although at its worst, his path couldn't hold a candle to the one she'd landed on. "Do you at least like it?"

"For the most part. There are days when I'd rather be in the mine."

"No offense," she told him, "but I'll take the bad day of a rich lawyer over the bad day of a poor maid anytime."

"Don't be so sure," he said. "You've never had to draft a prenuptial agreement for your step-grandmother."

At that moment, the girl at the counter called out their order, and he slid from the booth, leaving Patience to wonder about his answer. Writing some document hardly seemed a big ordeal.

Stuart returned a few minutes later with a tray laden with food. The smell of fresh beef made her stomach rumble. Grimy location or not, Al's did have good burgers.

She waited until they'd divided the burgers and French fries before picking up the conversation. "How is writing a prenuptial so awful?" she asked him. "It's not like unclogging a toilet or something."

"You wouldn't say that if you met Grandma Gloria."

"Harsh."

"Not harsh enough," he said, biting into his burger.

So Patience wasn't the only person Stuart had issues with. Maybe he didn't like outsiders in general. Or was it only women? "She had to have some redeeming quality. I mean if your grandfather loved her…"

"Grandpa Theodore *wanted* her. Big difference."

"She must have wanted him too," Patience replied. She wasn't sure why she felt the need to defend this Gloria person, unless it was because exonerating Gloria might improve her own standing in his mind.

"She wanted Duchenko money." There was no mistaking the venom in his voice. "And she went after it like a heat-seeking missile. Didn't matter who she got the money from, or who she had to hurt in the process."

Like who? The way his face twisted with bitterness made her think he was leaving something out of the story. It certainly explained why he had issues with her befriending Ana.

"This Gloria woman sounds lovely."

"Oh, she was a real peach. Did I mention she turned thirty-four on her last birthday?" he added abruptly.

"Thirty-four?"

"Uh-huh."

"Hasn't your grandfather been dead for…"

"Ten years," he supplied. My grandfather died ten years ago."

Making Gloria…ew. Patience wrinkled her nose at the image.

"Exactly. And now I'm stuck dealing with her for the rest of eternity."

Patience took a long sip of her cola. His comments had opened the door to a lot of questions, about many of which she had no business being curious, and yet seeing his frown, she couldn't help herself. "Ana doesn't talk much about her family," she said. "Other than you, that is.

"Unfortunately, there wasn't much love lost between Ana and Grandpa Theodore. From what I understand, they stopped speaking to each other around forty or fifty years ago. People were shocked when she traveled to his funeral. She told them it was only out of respect for me."

"Wow." To not speak to your sibling for decades? She couldn't imagine going more than two or three days without talking to Piper. "That must have been some fight."

"True. I asked Ana once, but all she said was Grandpa Theodore stole her happiness."

"How?" Ana seemed like one of the happiest people she knew.

"Beats me. I remember my father grumbling

once that he wished my grandfather would make things right this one time, so whatever happened was his fault. Unfortunately, unless Ana decides to open up, we might never know."

"Your poor dad. Sounds like he was stuck in the middle."

"For a little while anyway. He uh…" His eyes dropped to his half-eaten meal. "He and my mom died in a car accident when I was fourteen."

"Oh." Patience kicked herself for bringing up the subject. "I'm sorry."

"It was a long time ago."

Time didn't mean anything. There was nothing worse than having the ground yanked out from under you, leaving you with no idea where you belonged, what would happen next, or who would catch you if you fell. The teenage Stuart would have held in the pain, put on a strong face. She could tell by the way he held himself now, closed and protected.

Just like her. *No one should be forced to grow up before they're ready.*

Again, it was as if she'd spoken her thoughts

out loud, because Stuart looked up, his blue eyes filled with a mixture of curiosity and gratitude. "I'm going to go out on a limb and say you grew up earlier than I did."

His words twisted around her heart. If only he knew… For a crazy second, she longed to tell him everything, thinking that he, having been in her shoes, might understand. Reality quickly squashed her fantasy. He'd never understand. The two of them came from two different worlds. Rich versus poor. Clean versus dirty. Sitting here, sharing childhood losses, it was easy for that fact to slip her mind.

"It's not really a contest I wanted to win," she heard herself answer.

"I don't suppose anyone ever does." Picking up his soda, he saluted her with the paper cup. "To happier subjects."

That was it? No questions? No probing? Patience studied his face, looking for evidence that the other shoe was about to drop. She saw nothing but sincerity in his smoky eyes.

"To happier subjects," she repeated. She'd gotten off easy this time.

Or had she? Stuart smiled over the rim of his glass, causing her insides to flip end over end. All of a sudden, Patience didn't feel she'd gotten off at all. More like she was falling into something very dangerous.

"Ana seemed a little more with it tonight," Patience remarked a few hours later. They were walking along Charles Street on their way home from the hospital.

"Yes, she did," Stuart replied. The change from this afternoon made him hopeful. Interesting, how his aunt's improvement seemed tied to Patience's arrival. Much as he hated to admit it, the housekeeper and his aunt had a real rapport. Patience was so, well, patient, with the older woman. Gentle, too. Getting Ana water. Making her comfortable. Everything about Patience's behavior tonight screamed authenticity. If her kindness was an act, Patience deserved an award.

Then again, he'd seen award-worthy performances before, hadn't he? He'd purposely brought up Gloria over dinner to gauge Patience's reaction, thinking the topic of fortune hunters might at least cause her to reveal some kind of body language. Instead, he got sympathy, felt a connection…

"You're frowning." Patience remarked.

"Sorry, I was thinking how little Ana ate this evening."

"She never eats much. You know that."

Yes, thought Stuart, but he needed something to dodge her question.

They walked a few feet in silence. The night was balmy and clear. Combined with the warm breeze, it created an almost romantic feel to the air around them. Stuart stole a glance in Patience's direction. She had her arms folded across her chest, and her eyes were focused on the pavement. Even so, he could still sense the undulating of her hips. It was, he realized, unconscious and natural. Otherwise, he suspected she'd attempt to downplay the sensuality the way she did her figure and her looks. Hell, maybe she was trying and failing. She certainly wasn't having much luck minimizing the other two.

That plastic hair band was failing, too. Strands of hair had broken free, and covered her eyes. One of them needed to brush the bangs away so he could see their sparkle again.

He rubbed the back of his neck instead.

Patience must have mistaken the action for him being warm. "You can definitely tell it's going to be the first day of summer," she remarked.

"Longest day of the year. Did you know that after tomorrow, every day gets a few seconds shorter? Before you know it, we'll be losing two and a half minutes a day. Sorry," he quickly added. "I did a graph for a high school science fair. The fact kind of stuck with me."

"In other words, you were blind, asthmatic, unathletic and a science nerd. No wonder you gave up on baseball."

He felt his cheeks grow warm. "For the record, I'd outgrown the asthma by then."

"Glad to hear it."

"Hey, we can't all be homecoming queens."

If he didn't know better, he'd swear she hugged her body a little tighter. "I didn't go to many school dances," she said.

Another piece to what was becoming a very confusing puzzle. One moment she was sexy and sharp-witted; the next, her eyes reminded him of a kitten—soft and innocent. What the heck was her story? He was no closer to knowing if Patience had an agenda than he was this morning. They might say you get more flies with honey, but all he got was more questions.

Along with a dangerously mounting attraction.

Cool air greeted them upon entering the brownstone. Stuart shut the front door and turned on the hallway light. Nigel, who had been sitting on a table by the front window greeted them with a loud meow before running toward the kitchen.

"For crying out loud," Patience called after him. "It's only been a few hours."

At the other end of the hall, the meows grew louder and more indignant—if such a thing was possible. She rolled her eyes, earning a chuckle from Stuart. He said, "You think he's bad, you should have met the other Nigels."

There were more? "You mean he's not the first."

"Actually, he's the third. Nigel the Second lived here while I was in law school."

"Wow, Ana must really like the name Nigel." Either that or the woman wasn't very good at pet names.

"I asked her once why she gave them all the same name,' Stuart added. "She told me it was because they all have Nigel personalities."

"If that's true, remind me to avoid guys named Nigel."

Their chuckles faded to silence. Patience toed the pattern on the entryway carpet. What now? There was an awkward expectancy in the air, as if both of them knew they should do or say something. The problem was, neither knew what.

At least Nigel had stopped his meowing.

"Thank you for dinner,' she said finally.

"You're welcome." He smiled. "Maybe we've got this being civil thing down."

"Maybe. I have to admit, you're not bad company when you aren't accusing me of things."

"Never fear, tomorrow's another day," he replied. Patience would have laughed, but there was too much truth to his comment. This temporary truce of theirs could break at any time.

"By the way," he added, you're not such bad company yourself. When you aren't dodging questions."

"Like you said, tomorrow's another day." She turned to leave only to have her left foot tangle with something warm and furry. Nigel. She maneuvered herself awkwardly, trying to avoid stepping on the darn cat. Her ankle twisted, and she pitched sideways, toward the stairway. That caused her right knee to buckle, and before she knew it, she was falling in a heap.

Stuart caught her before her bottom touched the floor. "Stupid cat," she muttered.

"Are you okay?"

"I'm fine. Nigel on the other hand might have used up another one of his nine lives." She looked around, but the creature was nowhere to be found.

"He ran upstairs," Stuart replied, helping her to her feet.

"With his tail between his legs, I hope. If you didn't believe me before about Nigel causing Ana's fall, you have to believe me now."

"The evidence is definitely in your favor. Are you sure you're okay?"

"Positive. My butt didn't even hit the ground."

"Good. Hate to see you bruise something you might need," he said with a smile.

That's when she realized he still held her. His arm remained wrapped around her waist, pulling her close, so that their hips were flush. The odd angle gave Patience little choice but to rest her hand on his upper arm,

They might as well have been embracing.

He smelled of soap and laundry detergent. No aftershave—a testimony to his innate maleness that he didn't need anything more. Awareness—no, something stronger than awareness—washed over her, settling deep in the pit of her stomach.

Fingers brushed her bangs away from her temple. Barely a whisper of a touch, it shot straight to her toes. Slowly, she lifted her gaze. "I've been wanting to do that all night," he said in a voice softer than his touch.

"I—I'm growing out my bangs. That's why they keep falling in my face." Why did she think he wasn't talking about her bangs?

Maybe because his attention had shifted to her mouth. Staring, studying. Patience caught her lip between her teeth to stop it from trembling. All either of them needed to do was to move their head the tiniest bit and they would be close enough to kiss.

"I should check on Nigel…" She twisted from his grasp, combing her fingers through her hair in a lousy attempt to mask her abruptness. She needed to…she didn't know what she needed to do. The blood pounding in her ears made it hard to think.

She needed space. That's what. Turning on her heel, she headed upstairs, forcing herself to take one step at a time. She lasted until the second flight, when Stuart was out of sight, before doubling the pace.

Smooth going, Patience, she thought when she finally closed her bedroom door. Why don't you break out in a cold sweat while you're at it?

What on earth was wrong with her anyway? She'd dealt with literally dozens of unwanted advances over the years. Losers, pushy drunks, punks who couldn't keep their hands to themselves And she freaks out because Stuart touched her hair? The guy didn't even try anything.

Oh, but you wanted him to, didn't you? That's why she'd bolted. In spite of everything that had gone on between them in the past twenty-four hours, she actually wanted Stuart Duchenko to kiss her.

Heaven help her, but she still did.

CHAPTER FOUR

THE NEXT MORNING, Patience woke up with a far clearer head. Tossing and turning for half the night did that for a person.

When she thought things through, Patience wasn't really surprised that she was attracted to Stuart. Along with being handsome, he was the polar opposite of every man who had ever crossed her path. Sadly, that difference was exactly why she had no business kissing or doing anything else with him.

Throwing back the covers, she stretched and headed for the shower. Back in her and Piper's old apartment, a long hot shower was her way of scrubbing away life's dirt. The close, fiberglass stall had been her oasis. This morning, she was using Ana's Italian marble shower to rinse away last night's fantastical thoughts. There was probably some kind of irony in that. All she knew was she had to go back to keeping her distance before she made a fool of herself or, worse, said something she shouldn't.

The brownstone was empty when she finally came downstairs. A quick look toward his bedroom door—because she needed to prepare breakfast, not because she was thinking about him—showed Stuart was already awake. Up and out, apparently. A good thing, Patience told herself. She still wasn't sure how to explain her behavior last night, and Stuart's absence gave her the space she needed to come up with one.

Nigel was sitting by the kitchen door. The food littering his mat said he'd already had breakfast. There was coffee in the coffeepot, too.

"He sure is making it hard to stay unaffected, isn't he, Nigel?" She gave the cat a scratch behind the ear. "But we're going to do our best."

Just then the front door opened, signaling the end of her solitude. With a soft meow, Nigel trotted toward the entryway. "Hey, Nigel," she heard him greet. "Told you I'd be back."

Patience rubbed her arms, which had suddenly developed goose bumps. Amazing the way the air seemed to shift every time he entered a building. Like the atmosphere needed to announce his arrival.

And thank goodness, too. She turned to the door at the same time he entered, and if she hadn't been forewarned, her knees would have buckled underneath her completely.

He'd lied last night. No way the man walking into the kitchen was an unathletic nerd. His thin cotton tank might as well be nonexistent, the way it clung to his sweaty body. She could see every muscle, every inch of nonexistent fat. His arms alone…were lawyers allowed to have biceps that illegal? All those thoughts she had about his being commanding and superior? They doubled. And she'd thought he might kiss her last night? Talk about being a fool.

"Good morning." He barely looked in her direction as he made his way to the refrigerator. "Going to be a scorcher. You can feel the heat in the air already." Grabbing a bottle of water, he downed the contents in one long drink. "Did you sleep all right?"

Clearly last night's encounter hadn't affected him. "Fine," she lied, ignoring the hollow feeling threatening to take hold of her insides. "You?"

"As well as anyone with a furry bed warmer can sleep. Nigel has apparently appointed me the substitute Duchenko."

"I noticed you fed him. And made coffee. Thank you."

"Since I was awake first, it seemed only logical. Plus, Nigel would never have let me leave the house, and I wanted to get a run in before it got too humid."

"I didn't know you were a runner."

"Grandpa Theodore's idea. He thought it would help keep my lungs strong. The habit just sort of stuck." As he talked, he crossed the kitchen to the side where she stood. Patience gripped the counter a little tighter. Even sweaty, his skin smelled appealing. Instead of stale and dirty, it was the fresh, clean scent of exertion.

"I called the hospital before I left. Ana had a

good night," he said, reaching into the cupboard for a mug.

He offered her a mug, as well, but Patience shook her head. Sharing coffee together felt too domestic and familiar.

"Oh, good. I was thinking of taking her some of her favorite tea and cookies when I visited her today. Since you were concerned about her eating and all… what?"

He was giving her one of those looks, where he seemed to be trying to read her mind. "That's very thoughtful of you."

"You sound surprised."

"Actually…" His expression turned inward. "I'm beginning not to be."

"Thank you. I guess." Maybe he was finally realizing she wasn't some kind of criminal mastermind out to take his aunt's money or whatever it was he suspected her of being. Maybe this meant he would back off and her insides could unwind.

Or maybe not, she corrected, taking in his muscular arms.

"Don't get too comfortable. I'm still keeping an

eye on you." Damn, if the smile accompanying the remark didn't make her insides grow squirrelly. He finished pouring his coffee and headed toward the door. "I'm planning to stop by the hospital before work this morning. If you'd like, I can give you a ride."

"Thanks," she replied as Stuart left to get a shower. Sitting in close quarters with him while they wove through traffic was not her idea of fun. She'd bet he had a tiny Italian sports car so their knees could bump on every turn, too.

"Like I said," she remarked to Nigel, who had returned and was weaving in and out of her legs, "he's making it awfully difficult."

Stuart took the stairs two at a time. So much for the restorative powers of a good run. Five miles and his thoughts were still racing.

Not just his thoughts. All he could say was thank goodness Patience wasn't trying to look sexy or he'd have a heart attack.

It was time he accepted the fact that he'd gone from finding the woman attractive to being attracted to her. His fate was sealed the second his arm slipped around her waist. She fit so perfectly, her hips aligning with his as though they were meant to be connected...

Giving a groan, he kicked his bedroom door shut. It was all that damn tendril's fault. If the strand had stayed tucked in her band where it belonged, he wouldn't have been compelled to brush the hair from her face, and if he hadn't brushed her hair, he never would have considered kissing her.

And oh, did he consider. He owed her a thank-you for bolting upstairs. Kept him from crossing an improper line with his aunt's employee.

Raised a few more questions, too. Mainly, what made her flee in the first place? Stuart swore that for a few seconds before Patience took flight, he saw real desire in her eyes. Did she back off because she realized the mistake they were about to make or because of something more? The lady sure had her secrets.

Maybe he could find out what they were. That is, if he could keep his attraction—and his hands—to himself.

* * *

Surprisingly—or perhaps not so surprisingly—Patience left for the hospital without him. The hastily scrawled note pinned to the coffeemaker said she needed to stop at the tea shop to buy Ana her Russian caravan tea. "A reasonable excuse," he said to Nigel. But the tea shop was only a block away, and in the direction of the hospital. He would have gladly waited while she ran her errand.

No, more likely, she wanted to avoid being in the car with him. For him to care about her decision was silly, but care he did. Why didn't she want to ride with him?

Unfortunately, any answer had to wait because when he arrived at the hospital, his aunt was awake. Someone had raised her bed so she was sitting upright. Patience stood by her head, brushing out her hair. Stuart watched as her arm moved with long, slow strokes, each pass banishing the tangles of hospitalization. "Do you want to leave the braid down or wear it coiled?" he heard her ask.

"Coiled," Ana replied. "Of course."

He smiled. His aunt always insisted on looking as regal as possible. She was wearing the serenest of expressions. Her eyes were closed and the hint of a smile played across her lips. For the first time since he'd come home, she resembled the Ana he remembered.

His chest squeezed tight, his heart and lungs suddenly too big for his body. He was afraid to cough lest he spoil his aunt's moment.

"Good morning." The moment ended anyway, as Dr. Tischel, Ana's primary care physician boomed his greeting from behind his shoulder. *"Lapushka!"* Ana greeted with a smile. "How long have you been standing there?"

"Not long. I didn't want to disturb your beauty session." He locked eyes with Patience only to have her break the gaze and resume brushing. "How are you this morning, Tetya?" He kissed Ana's cheek.

"I don't know," she replied. "How am I, Karl?"

"Remarkably lucky, for one thing. You're too old to be rolling down staircases. We all are."

All the more reason not to stare at women two-thirds your age, thought Stuart. The good doctor's gaze had locked itself to a spot below Patience's neck. The housekeeper had angled her body toward the wall, but that didn't stop the man's blatant assessment.

"Will she be able to go home soon?" Stuart asked in a loud voice, drawing the man's attention. A question to which he already knew the answer, but then he wasn't asking because he wanted information.

"I'm afraid not," the doctor replied. The man didn't even have the decency to look embarrassed. "You took a nasty fall, Ana."

He lifted the sheet from where it covered the upper part of her legs. On the leg without a cast, a large bruise turned Ana's kneecap purple. Dr. Tischel touched around it, causing Ana to wince.

"Knee's pretty tender," he said, stating the obvious. "You're definitely going to have to stay off your feet for a little while."

"Are we talking about a wheelchair?" Stuart

asked. He was having trouble imaging his great-aunt managing crutches as the moment.

"At the very least," the doctor replied. "For a little while anyway."

"Don't worry," Patience said. "I'll push you around the house."

"Oh no, the brownstone has way too many stairs," Dr. Tishcel said. "That's what got you in trouble in the first place. The rehab hospital has a terrific orthopedics wing. They'll take good care of you."

"What?" In spite of her pain, Ana stiffened. "You're sending me to another hospital? For how long?"

"Depends," Dr. Tischel replied. "At least a couple of weeks."

"A couple weeks!" Patience and Ana spoke at the same time, although he was pretty sure their furor was for two different reasons. Stuart tensed at the announcement himself, and he'd been expecting the news since the day Ana fell. Two weeks sharing a house with Patience. Alone.

"I'm afraid so," Dr. Tischel replied. "We want

to make sure that ankle heals properly. I'll give them a call this afternoon and check on availability. With luck there's a bed open and we can transfer you tomorrow.

"In the meantime," he said, pulling the sheet back over her legs, "I want you to try and sit up in a chair for a few hours."

Ana gave an indignant cough. "Don't know why if I'm just going to be laid up in another hospital bed."

"Because the movement will do you good. You don't want to develop blood clots, do you?"

"No, she does not," Stuart answered. Seeing the doctor was getting ready to leave, he rose from his chair, hoping to keep the man from giving Patience another once-over. Granted, he shared Dr. Tischel's appreciation of her beauty, but the woman wasn't standing there for his viewing pleasure. He held out a hand. "Thank you for your help."

The gambit failed as the older man shook his hand only briefly before reaching across Ana to grasp Patience's. "It's my pleasure. Ana has always been one of my favorite patients."

Ana coughed again. "Favorite, my foot," she grumbled once the doctor left. "Stupid old fool wants to stick me in a nursing home."

"Rehab facility, Tetya." Stuart replied. Out of the corner of his eye, he caught Patience wiping her hand on her jeans. Apparently, she wasn't impressed with Dr. Tischel's behavior this morning, either. "It's only for a little while. You'll be back at the brownstone before you know it."

Ana shrugged. She looked so sad it made Stuart almost want to tell her Dr. Tischel had made a mistake. In a way, he understood. The news probably did sound like a sentence. She was losing her freedom.

He grabbed her fingers. "I'll visit every day, I promise."

"And me," Patience said. "I'll even find out if I can bring Nigel so you can see him, too."

"Will you?" Ana's face brightened. "I've been so worried about him. He acts tough, but on the inside, he's really very sensitive."

"I'll do everything I can. I promise."

Stuart watched while the two women talked about the cat, his chest squeezing tight again. The soft, caring tone in Patience's voice mesmerized him. She sounded so genuine; it made him want so badly to trust her intentions.

Could he?

Just then, Patience reached over to brush a strand of hair from Ana's face, sending his mind hurtling to the night before. Parts of his body stirred remembering how soft Patience's hair had felt sliding through his fingers. How on earth was he going to spend two weeks with Patience, get to know her and keep his attraction under control?

"Oh, no!"

Ana's cry shook him from his reverie. She sat straight, her face crumpled in distress. "What's wrong, Tetya?" he asked.

"The humane society dinner dance. I totally forgot, but it's tonight."

Was that all? Stuart let out his breath. "Looks like you'll have to miss this year's festivities."

"But I can't," Ana said. "I'm being honored

as the volunteer of the year. I'm supposed to be there to accept my award."

"I'm sure people will understand why you're not there, Tetya. You can have your friend, Mrs. Calloway, accept on your behalf."

"Ethyl Calloway is not my friend," his aunt snapped.

Stuart should have remembered. Ana and Ethyl weren't friends so much as friendly society rivals. The two of them had worked side by side at the Beacon Hill Humane Society for years, competing to see who could do more to further the organization's good work. As a result, hundreds of homeless cats and dogs had found new homes. Personally, he thought it incredibly fitting that Ethyl accept the award on his aunt's behalf, but what did he knew?

"Missing the ceremony isn't going to diminish what you've done for the shelter," Patience said. "People will still know about your hard work."

To Patience's credit, her comment worked. Ana settled back against her pillow, her agitation fading. "Will you accept the award for me?" she asked.

Stuart cringed. The humane society dinner dance was a nightmare of society women and their spouses who made it their mission to offer up single granddaughters to every eligible bachelor who had the misfortune of attending. Those without granddaughters used their time to strong-arm donations. The last time Ana had convinced him to attend, he'd left four figures poorer and with a pocket full of unwanted phone numbers. But the organization was Ana's pride and joy. Accepting her award was the least he could do.

"Of course I will," he told her.

His aunt and Patience exchanged an odd look. "What?" he asked.

"I think she meant me," Patience said.

The blush coloring her cheeks couldn't be as dark as the one heating his. "Oh. I didn't…"

"I had no idea you'd be home this week," his aunt said, her eyes looking deeply apologetic, "and you know how I hate to attend alone."

"You're more than welcome to go in my place," Patience added. "I don't mind."

No kidding. Her eyes were practically begging him to say yes, they were so hopeful-looking.

Unable to see the silent exchange, Ana waved the offer away. "Nonsense. You never go out. This is your chance to dress up and have a good time. Stuart will go with you."

"I will?" The painkillers had to be making Ana loopy again. Take Patience to an event where holding her in his arms would be encouraged? Bad idea.

"Someone has to keep the men from pestering her," Ana said. "You know how persistent some of those people can be."

Yes he did. In that sea of gray hair and pearls, Patience was going to stand out like a star. A welcome distraction for every senior man there.

Stuart wasn't sure if what he felt was jealousy or wariness on their behalf. "Ana's got a point," he said. "There is no reason why we shouldn't go together."

"See, dear? Stuart's on board.

He could see the moment Patience accepted her fate. Her shoulders slumped ever so slightly and she nodded. "All right."

"Good, it's settled. Stuart will go with you to the dance, then tomorrow you can both fill me in on all the gossip." Ana relaxed a little more, the smile from earlier returning to her face.

"If you don't want to attend together, I'll understand," Stuart said when they stepped into the corridor a short while later. "I know Ana backed you into a corner. I'll be glad to deal with these people on my own."

Why? Was he trying to do her a favor or did he think she wouldn't fit in at the society function? Patience had to admit the second question had crossed her mind more than once.

She also had to admit that Ana hadn't backed her into anything. As soon as she suggested Stuart go along, her entire body broke out in excited tingles. Which, now that she thought about it, was a far bigger problem than not fitting in. Unfortunately…

"It's too late to back out now. Ana's expecting a report from both of us."

Patience wished she could read what was behind Stuart's long sigh. He ran a hand over his features, and when he finished, the face he revealed was an expressionless mask. "Very well," he said. "We'll go, collect her award, and make it an early night. That way, neither of us has to spend more time at this party than necessary."

Good idea, thought Patience. Less time for her to get into trouble.

So why did she feel disappointed?

CHAPTER FIVE

PATIENCE SMOOTHED THE front of her dress, then smoothed it again. Why hadn't she gone shopping this afternoon when she had the chance? The little black dress she pulled out of the closet was too short, too tight and too tacky. Everything about her screamed *cheap*.

It hadn't mattered when she'd thought she was attending with Ana. Or maybe it hadn't mattered *as much*. While naturally she wanted to please Ana, the older woman didn't make her stomach tumble.

Stuart shouldn't either, remember?

A knock sounded on her door. "Patience?" So much for not affecting her stomach. The sound of his voice made the butterflies' wings beat faster.

She draped a scarf around her shoulders, hoping that the draped material might camouflage her cleavage, smoothed her dress one more time and slipped into her pumps.

The heels were way too high. Would anyone notice how banged up her black flats were?

"Patience?"

Face it, she'd look out of place no matter what she wore. Best she could do was wear a smile and hope Stuart wasn't too horrified by her appearance.

Taking a deep breath, she opened the door.

Afraid of what she might see in Stuart's face, she avoided raising her eyes past his torso. That view was intimidating enough as it was. He was in full lawyer mode in a black suit similar to the one she remembered from the emergency room. This time, he finished off the outfit with a blue tie, the color of his eyes. To her embarrassment, Patience noticed her scarf matched. Made them look coordinated. *Like a couple.*

Maybe he wouldn't notice.

"Sorry to keep you waiting," she said.

"No worries. It was…worth the wait." There was an odd hitch to his voice. Mortification, maybe? Still afraid to look up and see, she pretended to pay attention to the steps as they headed downstairs.

"The Landmark isn't too far from here," he said. "Would you like to walk or drive?"

Once again, she faced the specter of being in a dark closed space with him. "Would you mind walking? I could use the fresh air." Anything to get the butterflies to settle down.

"Are you sure?" She didn't need to ask to know he was referring to her high heels. If only he knew how many hours she'd logged in shoes like these. A few blocks' walk would be a piece of cake.

The night air was surprisingly comfortable. A gentle breeze greeted them as they stepped onto the stoop. While Stuart locked the door behind them, Patience looked up at the darkening sky. A handful of early stars twinkled hello, and she made a quick wish that the night would turn out all right. Remembering their conversation from the night before, she asked, "How much daylight did we lose today?"

Stuart chuckled. "None, actually. The drop in daylight doesn't start for a few more days."

"So yesterday's explanation was wrong?"

"Generalized. I didn't realize I was going to be quizzed."

His hand hovered by the small of her back, guiding her down the steps. Patience made sure to walk quickly so as to avoid contact. "I'm sorry Ana strong-armed you into coming with me."

"I thought we covered this at the hospital. She strong-armed both of us."

"Yeah, but still I thought I should apologize. To be honest, I'm surprised you haven't said anything about the fact she and I were going together. I thought for sure you'd comment on it being part of my agenda."

"I thought about it, but since I know how badly Ana likes to have someone attend these things with her, 'll give you a pass." He flashed a smile. "Don't get used to it, though."

Patience added it to her list. Right after "going to parties with Stuart."

They stopped to wait for the traffic light. "I've

never been to one of these kinds of events before," she said, while they waited for the light to change. "Any chance they'll present Ana's award early?"

"Nope. They need incentive for people to stick around. How else would they get them liquored up enough to bid on the silent auction items?"

"You ever bid?"

"Are you kidding? Those society women are worse than mob enforcers. You'd be amazed at the stuff they've convinced me to bid on. And for how much."

Patience fought a smile picturing Stuart fending off a parcel of senior citizens. "Did you win?"

"Twice. Once I won a gym membership. That was useful. The other time it was a romantic getaway to Newport, Rhode Island."

"Romantic weekend, huh?" She fought back the intense curiosity that rose up with his answer. Who was the lucky woman? In her mind, she pictured someone smart and sophisticated and who always wore the perfect outfit. Since his dating life wasn't her business, she settled for the blandest response she could think of. "At least you won something fun."

"So my secretary said."

"You took her on the trip?"

"No, I gave it to her as a bonus. She took her husband."

There was no need to feel relieved, but she was anyway.

They reached the Landmark just as a limousine pulled to the front door and a couple stepped on to the curb. Seeing the way the woman's diamond cocktail ring sparkled from a block away, Patience's palms began to sweat. She was supposed to mingle with these people? What was she going to talk about with them? By the way, what furniture polish does your cleaning lady use?

"Hey, you okay?"

She nodded, and adjusted her scarf. "I'm glad you're here is all. I'm a little…" Why not admit the truth? "I'm a little out of my league."

"Why?" he said. "It's just a lot of people dressed up and showing off."

A lot of people who hired people like her. No,

correction. Who hired cleaning ladies. They wouldn't let her in the door, let alone hire her, if they knew her story.

"What you should really worry about is whether the chicken will be any good." His hand molded to the small of her back. The warmth of his touch spread up her spine, giving her courage. It was only for a few hours. She could do this.

The couple they saw were waiting for the elevator when they entered the lobby. It took less than ten seconds for Patience's confidence to flag. The same amount of time it took for the husband to smile and check out her legs. She wished Stuart's hand was still on her back. Then she could pretend he was with her by choice, and, by extension, the entire room would think so too. Instead, his fingers barely brushed her as they boarded the elevator.

Ethyl Calloway greeted them at the ballroom door. She was a tall, handsome woman who, like their companion on the elevator, was decorated with expensive jewelry. "Stuart! It's so good to see you." She kissed the air by his cheek. "How is Anastasia doing?"

"Much better," Stuart replied. "Already chomping at the bit to get back to her volunteer schedule. We had to practically tie her to the bed to keep her in the hospital."

"Well, at her age, it's best she not push herself too soon."

Her age? Ethyl wasn't much younger. The way the corner of Stuart's mouth was fighting not to smile, he was thinking the same thing. "Knowing Ana, she'll recover so fast she'll make the rest of us look lazy," Patience said.

Ethyl looked over as though she was noticing her for the first time. "Hello—Patty, isn't it?"

"Patience."

"Right. Ana mentioned she gave you a ticket. I'm glad you could make it. You'll be accepting Ana's award for her, right?" The older woman turned her attention back to Stuart. Actually, she physically turned toward Stuart and, in doing so, turned her back to Patience. Not on purpose, she told herself. Even so, she found herself blocked from the conversation. While Stuart nodded and went over details, she stood awkwardly to the side, smiling at the people who glanced in her direction.

"Lucky us," Stuart said, once Ethyl freed him from her attentions. "We're sitting at the front table."

"What does that mean?" From his sarcasm, she guessed not anything good.

"We get our rubber chicken first."

"Oh."

"And we get to sit with Ethyl. Take good notes. Ana's going to want a blow-by-blow recap." He pointed across the crowd to a congregation in the corner. "Looks like the bar is over there. I'll buy you drink."

They wound their way through the crowd, a difficult task as every ten feet some acquaintance of Ana's stopped them to ask for a medical update. After one very familiar-looking man inquired, she touched Stuart's arm. "Was that…?"

"The mayor?" He nodded.

Yep, she was out of her league. Please don't let me do something stupid

"Wine?" Stuart asked when they finally reached the front of the bar line.

Patience shook her head. "Sparkling water, please." Alcohol would go straight to her head, and she needed to keep her senses as sharp as possible. Another man walked by and checked out her legs. She gave the hemline a tug, on the off chance she could cover another quarter inch or so.

"You look fine." Stuart's breath was gentler than the breeze as he bent close and whispered in her ear. "Just a bunch of people..."

"Dressed up and showing off." She repeated his lesson for his benefit. Certainly her insides weren't listening. Her skin crawled, positive she was being evaluated by every person in the room and coming up short. What was that phrase about putting lipstick on a pig?

How she envied Stuart and the effortlessness with which he fit into his world. "I bet you go to a lot of these kinds of parties," she said to him.

"Only when I absolutely have to. Crowds and parties aren't really my thing."

"Really? But you look so at home." Everyone did, except for her.

"I'll tell you a secret." He leaned in close again. Damn, if he didn't smell better than the flower arrangements. "It helps if you think of all this as one big game," he said.

Distracted by the way his lips moved when he whispered, Patience nearly missed what Stuart said. "A game?"

"One big contest. Society's version of who's the biggest. Everyone's trying to prove they're better than the other."

"You make it sound like the whole room is a big pile of insecurity."

"Isn't it?"

"Including you?" she asked, although she couldn't imagine Stuart ever having a reason to be insecure.

"I've had my moments. Hard not to when you're raised by Theodore Duchenko." His eyes looked down at the glass in his hand, studying the contents. "My grandfather would make anyone feel insecure. He was what you'd call 'larger than life.'"

She was beginning to think life under Theodore Duchenko wasn't much of a picnic. "And step-grandma?"

A shadow crossed his features. It might have been a shadow from one of the people in the crowd, but Patience couldn't be sure. Whatever it was, the passing left his expression darker than before. "Gloria is a case unto herself."

What did that mean? Before she could ask, he was steering her toward a group of tables lining the side wall on which were displayed a collection of wrapped baskets, photographs and other items. "The infamous silent auction," Stuart announced. "Everything a person couldn't want, dutifully accompanied by a heaping serving of guilt." He pointed to an easel next to the table where a large poster sat. Above the photograph of a big black Labrador, a caption read, "He's got so much love to give; if only someone would love him back." The dog's big brown eyes grabbed Patience's heart and squeezed.

"Admit it," Stuart said. "You want to adopt a puppy now, don't you. Or at least bid on a membership to the wine-of-the-month club." Patience took a long drink from her glass. The puppy and the wine weren't the only things she wanted and couldn't have.

The two of them spent time reviewing the various items up for auction, with Stuart predicting how much he thought the final bid would be for each one. Despite his sarcastic commentary, he too bid on a few items, including a customized kitty tree for Nigel and, to Patience's surprise, a braided gold bracelet. "This is for Ana right?" she teased. "Because I'm not sure your assistant's husband would like you giving his wife jewelry."

"Who says I wasn't planning to give the bracelet to you?"

She laughed. Wistful quivers aside, that was hardly likely. "Exactly what you give the girl you don't trust."

"You don't think I would?"

"I think…" His eyes dared her to believe his offer. "I hope you're joking," she said.

"You're not into expensive jewelry?"

Not if it came with strings attached, and that was the only kind of expensive jewelry she knew of. "I think Ana would enjoy the gift more."

There was something very off-putting about the way he reacted to her response. Rather than laugh or look disappointed, he gave her one of those soul-searching stares.

She was about to ask him if she'd said something wrong when Ethyl Calloway reappeared with a silver-haired gentleman behind her. "This is Bernard Jenkins from WZYV," she said, stepping in front of Patience—again. "He's emceeing tonight's award presentation. Since you're accepting Anastasia's award, I thought you two should meet."

On the emcee's arm was the most statuesque blonde Patience had ever seen without a stripper pole.

The woman introduced herself as a Natalie Something. "We met last year at the bar's program on the revised probate laws," she said, pumping Stuart's hand with enthusiasm.

"That's right," Stuart replied. "You're with Ropes Prescott. Good to see you again."

The conversation moved into a mishmash of names and companies Patience didn't know. She could see why Bernard became a deejay. The man knew how to talk. And talk. Patience put on a pretend smile and used the time to examine the lovely Natalie. Her little black dress was current. In fact, Patience was pretty sure she'd seen a picture of the dress in a fashion magazine last month. The woman knew all the "in" jokes too. Every time she laughed, she would toss her mane of blond curls and let her fingers linger on Stuart's jacket sleeve. Patience squeezed her glass. She'd wanted to know what kind of woman Stuart would date. She had a pretty good idea now. Her stomach soured.

Meanwhile, Bernard Jenkins gave her a wink.

"Excuse me," she murmured. Without bothering to see if anyone heard her, she slipped away in search of a few quiet moments in the ladies' room. The draped tables used for guest check-in were empty save for a solo volunteer who was packing unused papers into a box. She smiled as Patience walked by, the first smile she'd received outside of Stuart's all night.

"People dressed up and showing off," she repeated to herself. Was it really all a game, like Stuart said? If so, he had to be one of the winners. It was so obvious when you compared him to everyone else in the room.

"Isn't this a pleasant surprise."

Dr. Tischel came strolling out of the ballroom, with a smile as broad as the rest of him. "Twice in one day. Fortune must be smiling on me."

"Hello, Dr. Tischel."

"Karl, please." Spreading his arms, he drew her into an unexpected hug. Pulling her close, he held on so tightly Patience had to angle her spine to prevent his hips from pressing against hers. Antiseptic and cologne assaulted her nostrils, making her grimace.

After a beat longer than necessary, she managed to extricate herself. "Is Mrs. Tischel here, too?"

"Last I heard she was in Salem with all the other witches." He laughed at his joke.

Patience took a step backward. His eyes had that glassy sheen she knew too well. She looked to the check-in table, hoping the volunteer might help, but the woman had conveniently disappeared. And she could forget Stuart. He was probably so busy talking to the lovely Natalie he didn't realize she was missing. Looked like she would have to deal with the situation the same way she'd solved problems her whole life. On her own.

She took another step backward. Distance was always the first solution. "Ana was looking better when I left her this afternoon." A safe topic always helped, too.

"Ana? Oh, Ana." He waved a sloppy hand through the air. "She's a tough old bird. Are you here alone?"

Thank goodness, a way out of this conversation without causing a scene. "No, I'm here with Ana's nephew, Stuart. In fact, he's probably—"

"The one whose girlfriend dumped him?"

"I wouldn't know anything about that," she replied. Other than thinking that if true, the woman was a fool. "I should be getting back—"

The doctor grabbed her upper arm, preventing her from passing. "Let me buy you a drink."

His hot, stale breath made her want to gag. "No." Shoving the man with enough force that he tottered sideways, she broke free and hurried back into the ballroom.

A half dozen pairs of eyes turned in her direction. Of course. Pay attention now, after she no longer needed anyone's assistance. Wasn't that always the way? For crying out loud, but she was tired of being stared at. She looked down at her dress. Her scarf had been pushed aside during her scuffle with Dr. Tischel, revealing her ample cleavage for all the world to see. No wonder the good doctor had hit on her. She looked like a two-bit hooker.

"There you are."

The crowd parted and there was Stuart threading his way through the guests, his eyes glittering with a different kind of brightness. One that suggested he was actually glad to see her. "I was wondering where you went. Is everything all right?"

He was looking her up and down, taking in the disheveled scarf and goodness knows what else. "What happened?"

"Nothing." Patience didn't want to talk about it. Her arm hurt from where Dr. Tischel had grabbed her, and she was starting to get a headache. "I'm not feeling well is all."

He arched a brow. Why, she didn't know. She was telling the truth. She didn't feel well. "I'm—"

As if on cue, Dr. Tischel lurched by them, his shoulder striking her shoulder blade and pitching her forward. Stuart caught her by the arms before she crashed into him.

"We meet again," the doctor said. A lewd smile unfurled across his face as his eyes locked onto her exposed neckline.

In a flash, Stuart was between them, blocking the doctor's line of sight. "Maybe you should get some coffee," he said, his tone making it clear he didn't expect an argument. When the doctor had left, Stuart turned back to face Patience. "Are you all right?"

Everyone was looking at them. Patience could feel the stares on her skin, worse than before. A tiny sob escaped before she could stop it. "No," she said.

"Come on." A warm arm wrapped itself around her shoulder and guided her toward the door. "Let's get some air."

Stuart led her to an unused conference room down the hall. There weren't any chairs, but it was private. "Was he the reason you wanted to leave?"

"I ran into him outside and he got a little grabby."

"Jeez. What is it with old guys and young girls? Did he hurt you?"

"No. I'm fine." Wrapping her arms around her body, she stared out the window at the traffic on Newbury Street. She hated that she let Dr. Tischel's leering get to her. The old guy was no worse than any of the others. "I thought these people would be different."

"Different how?"

"Better, I suppose. Stupid, I know." She should have known better.

Stuart joined her at the window. His nearness made her feel warm and safe, and, while she knew she shouldn't, Patience let the sensation surround her. "Sometimes I wonder if I'll ever be more than a hot body to people."

"Hey—you are more." Gripping her shoulders, he forced her to turn around and look at him. "Way more."

If he knew how dangerously good his words made her feel... "Not to guys like Dr. Tischel," she said. As far as she knew, there were way more of his kind than anyone else.

"Dr. Tischel is a drunken moron," Stuart replied "In fact, first thing tomorrow, I'm going to talk to Ana about switching physicians. A guy who drinks like that? I don't want him anywhere near her."

"Can we not tell her about the grabbing part? I don't want to upset her."

"I suppose that means punching him out on the dance floor is out of the question too?"

He was being purposely outrageous, and it worked. Patience smiled. "Yes, it is."

"Too bad. It'd be fun to watch the old guy fall. Nice to see you smiling again though. There's nothing worse than seeing a pretty woman looking sad. I can say you're pretty, right?"

Color flooded her cheeks. He could say anything he wanted. The man had her completely under his spell at the moment. "Thank you," she said.

"For what?"

"Being so nice. You didn't have to be." It was true. He could have let her go home in a taxi cab and wiped his hands of her. Instead, here he was making her feel…special.

"What can I say? Didn't you watch me at the silent auction table? I'm a sucker for sad brown eyes."

Patience tried to blush again, but fingers caught her chin, forcing her to hold his gaze. "I can't help myself."

"Sorry." She couldn't think of another response, her brain having short-circuited as soon as he touched her. The connection reached far deeper than her skin. Stuart didn't know it, but he was the first person besides Piper to ever talk to her this way, as if she was a person, whole and worthwhile. Cracks formed in the wall she'd so carefully built to keep the world from closing in.

"Don't be." His touch shifted, fingers tracing their way along her jaw and across her cheek. Patience knew exactly what he was tracing. Like so much about her, the jagged line could be covered but never completely erased. She'd cut herself falling off a table. A painful reminder of what happened when a person got too close.

Stuart was breaking that rule right now. Scary as the thought was, she longed to sink into his touch.

"You still want to go back to the brownstone?" he asked.

"No,"

"Good." One word, but it—and the smile that

came along—made her feel more wanted than all the words in the dictionary could.

The cracks grew wider.

He held out his hand. "Let's go get Ana her award."

Stuart still wanted to punch Karl Tischel in the nose. What was it with rich old men and young women—did they think that every woman belonged to them?

Or just the women Stuart was with?

Thinking of how many times he'd caught Tischel leering at Patience, his fingers curled into a fist. Three strikes and you're out, Doc.

When had the fight become so personal? Was it when she'd answered her bedroom door looking like an eleven-point-five on a ten-point scale? Or when he saw her walk into the ballroom pale and shaken? When had he gone from being attracted to the woman to caring about her feelings? Damn if her likability wasn't getting to him, too.

They managed to get through dinner and the awards presentation without incident. Unless you counted Bernard Jenkins's pompous droning. Honestly, did the man ever come up for air? The guy spent the entire meal giving Patience and Ethyl a grape-by-grape account of his recent trip to the Tuscan vineyards.

Bernard's date, Natalie, wasn't much better. When she wasn't agreeing with Bernard, she was laughing and tossing her hair as though every word Stuart said was the most fascinating thing she'd ever heard. The woman reminded him of Gloria. Continually on the lookout for a brighter horizon. Aging local celebrity or rich lawyer. Nerdy law student or elderly silver magnate. They made their decisions based on whatever put them on top.

Ethyl was at the podium announcing the winners of the silent auction when a flash of movement caught his eye. Turning, he saw Patience texting away on her cell phone. Suspicion tried to take hold but failed. Tonight, he was suspicioned out.

"I'm sending Ana a picture of you accepting her award," she said when she noticed he was watching.

"I don't think she's awake at this hour."

"No, but this way she'll see it first thing in the morning, and I get extra brownie points." Her smile knocked the wind from his lungs.

"And finally, the gold bracelet donated by Basmati Jewelers was won by Paul Veritek." A smattering of applause floated across the room.

"You didn't win," Patience said. "Sorry."

"I'll live." He wasn't sure what had possessed him to bid on the bracelet in the first place. Seeing Patience's bare wrists had him offering up a bid without thinking. In a room filled with expensive jewelry, the simplicity stood out. But then, she didn't need jewelry, or makeup for that matter, to stand out, did she?

"And that concludes our program," Ethyl announced. "We look forward to seeing you next year."

"Guess that means the evening is over," Patience said.

"All but the dancing." Right on schedule, a Big Band standard began to play. As he watched couples making their way to the dance floor,

Stuart was suddenly gripped with the desire to join them.

"Feel like dancing?"

"I thought you said you wanted to leave right after the ceremony."

He did. He also told himself putting his arms around Patience again was the worst idea ever, but now he couldn't think of anything he'd rather do. "I changed my mind. A few dances might be fun."

"I—" He'd caught her off guard, and she was struggling with what to say. The hesitancy made his palm actually start to sweat like a high schooler.

"Okay," she said finally. "Why not?"

His thrill over her acceptance was like a high schooler's, too.

He led her to the far edge of the dance floor, where the crowd wouldn't swallow them up, and pulled her close. Last night's embrace had been tentative and accidental, but here on the dance floor, he was free to hold her as close and for as long as he liked.

They moved in sync, their bodies slipping together in a perfect fit. Not surprisingly, Patience moved with a natural rhythm, her lower half moving back and forth like the waves in an ocean. Or like a lover meeting his thrusts. Stuart rested his hand on her hip and savored every shift beneath his fingers.

The song ended, and another ballad began. And another. They danced and swayed until the deejay announced it was time to say good-night.

Patience lifted her head from his shoulder. Her eyes were as bright as he'd ever seen then, with a sheen that looked suspiciously like moisture. "Thank you for chasing Dr. Tischel out of my head," she whispered.

That was all it took. Something inside him started to fall.

They walked up Beacon Street in silence, both of them pretending to act matter-of-fact even though they both knew their relationship had changed. How and why could wait until later. Right now, Stuart was content listening to the click-clack of Patience's heels on the sidewalk and reliving the feel of her curves beneath his hands. As for Patience, she was letting her fingers glide along the fence lining Boston Public Garden. "A fancy cake for Mrs. F," she said in singsongy tone under her breath.

"Whose Mrs. F?" he asked.

She flashed him a nostalgic-looking smile. "It's from a bedtime story I used to read to Piper about a man delivering cakes around Boston. A fancy cake for Mrs. F who lived on Beacon Hill. I think of the line whenever I see this row of houses."

Another memory involving raising her sister. Interesting how easily she shared those memories yet said so little about her own childhood. Beyond what he'd pulled out of her over dinner, that is. It was as if she didn't have a childhood of her own, Considering the shadows he'd seen in her eyes last night, maybe she hadn't.

So many pieces of her he didn't understand, so many parts unrevealed.

The story she described was one you read to a young child. "How old is your sister anyway?"

"Piper? Twenty-two."

Eight years younger. "So you read your sister a bedtime story when you were a kid?"

There was a stutter in her step. "Yeah, I did."

"I'm guessing your mom worked nights."

"Um…not really. She was just…busy." The evasiveness had returned, only this time what she didn't say came through loud and clear. If he had to guess, he'd say she'd started raising Piper long before their mother passed away. A child raising a child. He'd been right; she hadn't had a childhood of her own. She *was* like those damn dogs on the humane society poster, only instead of sympathy or guilt twisting in his gut, he wanted to wrap Patience in his arms and hold her tight and tell her she never had to be on her own again.

"I'm—"

"Don't." Stepping in front of him, she cut him off. "You're about to say you're sorry, and I don't want the sympathy."

"Okay, no sympathy." He understood. Sympathy was too much like pity. "How about admiration?"

"How about nothing? I did what I had to do. Trust me, I didn't do anything special," she said, turning away.

Except that Stuart didn't trust her, or had she forgotten? Had he forgotten for that matter?

They kept walking until they reached the State House, the moon reflecting off its golden dome. Around the corner, Stuart spotted a trio of staggering silhouettes making their way from Park Street station. Patience was walking a few feet ahead. Her curves made her the perfect target for drunken comments. Stepping up his pace, he positioned himself on her right, creating a buffer. The group came closer, and he saw that two of the three were women teetering on high heels. The pair clung to the shoulders of the man in the middle, a pasty-looking blond who looked like he spent most of his time in dimly lit places. Their raucous laughter could be heard from ten feet away.

Stuart stole a look in Patience's direction before

slipping his arm around her waist. She looked back, but didn't say anything.

As luck would have it, the trio reached the signal light the same time as they did. The man made no attempt to hide his ogling. "Come join the pah-ty, baby," he slurred, alcohol making his Boston accent thicker. "We're gonna go all night."

Patience's body turned rigid. He tightened his grip on her waist, letting her know he'd keep her safe.

The drunk slurred on, oblivious. "This dude knows what I'm talking about, doncha? Life's too short. Gotta grab the fun while you can. I did." He slapped one of the women on the rear, and she let out a giggly yelp. "Me and these ladies are just getting started."

Just then, a public works truck drove up, its bright headlights lighting their slice of the street.

"Oh, my God," one of the women cried out. "I know you!" Pushing herself free, she stumbled closer, her oversize breasts threatening to burst free from her tiny camisole top. "You work at Feathers. I danced right after you. Chablis, remember?"

Patience didn't reply. She stared straight ahead. When the light changed, she stepped off the curb and started walking. Stuart had to step quickly to keep up.

"What's the matter, you too good to talk to me now? That it?" Chablis asked as she followed. "Hey, I'm talkin' to you."

A crimson-nailed hand reached out to grab Patience's shoulder, but she quickly turned and dodged the woman's touch. "You have the wrong person," she hissed.

When they reached the opposite side of the street, Chablis looked to make one more attempt at conversation only to have her friend tug her in the opposite direction. "Come on, baby," he slurred. "We don't need them. We got better things to do."

"Yeah, Chablis," the other woman whined. "Give it up. That witch ain't owning up to nuthin'."

"But I know her," Chablis insisted, as if her

knowledge was the most important discovery in the world. As she let her friends drag her away, she continued to swear and complain about being ignored. "She always did think she was better than us," Stuart heard her mutter.

"Sorry about that," he said to Patience.

"It's no big deal. They're just a bunch of drunks."

Perhaps, but the pallor of her skin said they'd upset her more than she let on. Poor thing had probably had her fill of drunks by this point.

A beer can came hurtling in their direction, rattling the sidewalk a few feet shy of where they stood. "Hey!" Chablis yelled, her voice sharp in the night. "Does your boyfriend know he's dating a stripper?"

Stuart might have laughed if Patience hadn't stopped in her tracks. When he looked, he saw the color had drained from her face.

A sick feeling hit him in his stomach. "She's got you confused with someone else, right?" he asked.

Even in the dark of night, Patience's eyes told

him everything he needed to know. There was no mistake.

Chablis was telling the truth.

CHAPTER SIX

"IT'S TRUE, ISN'T IT?" he asked. "You were a—a…"

Stripper? He couldn't even say the word, could he?

Stupid Chablis. Patience never did like the woman. For a second, she considered blaming everything on the rambling of a drunken trio, but one look at Stuart's face snuffed that idea. The thought had been planted in his head, and no amount of denial would chase it away. Eventually, he would dig up the truth. No reason to drag the ordeal out longer than necessary.

How stupid for her to think the night would end on a good note. Like she would ever earn a fairy-tale ending.

Folding her arms across her chest, Patience held on to what little dignity she could. "We prefer the term 'exotic dancer,'" she said, pushing her way past him.

"Where do you think you're going?"

"Where do you think? To the brownstone to pack my things." With luck she would get there before the tears pressing the back of her eyes broke free. Now that Stuart knew about her background, he was bound to ask her to leave her job with Ana. Hadn't he said that he didn't want Dr. Tischel anywhere near his aunt. Surely he would feel the same about Patience.

Well, she might have just lost her job, and her home, but she would not lose her composure—not on the streets of Boston and not in front of him.

There were footsteps, and Stuart was at her shoulder, grabbing her arm much like Dr. Tischel had. With a hiss, she pulled away. The look of regret passing over his features was small compensation.

"You're not even going to try and explain yourself?"

Patience had never felt more dirty and exposed

as she did under his stare, but she managed to hold herself together. "Why should I? You don't want to listen." No, he would judge her like everyone else had. The same way she judged herself. Why stick around to listen to condemnations she'd said to herself?

Stuart blocked her path. "Try me." Between the shadows and his stony expression, it was impossible to read his thoughts

They weren't the words she had expected to hear, and Patience hated how they made her heart speed up with hope. "You're really willing to listen?"

"I said I would. Don't you think you owe us an explanation?"

Us, as in him and Ana. With the shock of discovery wearing off, guilt began to take hold. She owed Ana way more than an explanation, but the truth was a good place to start. "Fine, but not here. Please." Out of the corner of her eye, she caught the silhouette of a person standing in a window. "I'll tell you everything when we're at the brownstone." Then she'd move out and never bother him or Ana again.

Neither said a word the final few blocks. Such a different silence compared to when they had left the hotel. Then, the air had hummed with romantic possibility. This long walk was nothing but cold.

Naturally Nigel was waiting for their return, meowing and running back and forth for attention. Without a word, they walked into the kitchen so she could give Nigel his midnight snack. Attending to a cat's needs had never taken so long.

"You ready to talk?" he asked when she'd finished rinsing the can.

"Not much to say." She'd already decided to give him the shortest version possible. Less misery that way. "I needed money and dancing was the only job I could find that would pay me enough."

Minus the part where she turned down the offer twice before finally giving in, and only then because her creepy boss at the burger place wouldn't give her more hours unless she slept with him.

"Interesting." He pulled out a chair and motioned for her to take a seat. "Now how about you give me the full version?"

The full version? Her heart hitched. She'd never told anyone the *whole* story. "Why do you care about the details? It is what it is."

"Because I care." The words warmed her insides, until she reminded herself he meant "about the details." He was, after all, a lawyer. Naturally, he'd want to collect all the facts.

Question was—how many facts did he need? She'd buried so much of her story that even she wasn't sure of everything anymore.

Taking a seat, she wiped the dampness from her palms on her dress. "Where do you want me to start?"

"Try the beginning."

"I was born."

"I'm serious."

"So am I." Where *did* she begin? "I suppose everything really started when Piper was born.

My mom—don't get me wrong, she wasn't a horrible mother. I mean, she didn't beat us or let us starve or anything like that. She just wasn't into being a mom, you know?"

A quick look across the table said he didn't, but she plowed ahead. "I think she thought a baby would keep Piper's dad around, but…"

She shrugged. That was her mother's pipe dream, not hers. "Anyway, as soon as I got old enough, she left taking care of Piper to me. But I told you that already."

"'A fancy cake for Mrs. F,'" he recited. "How old were you?"

"Twelve or thirteen? Thirteen, I think. It wasn't that hard," she added quickly. As was the case whenever a person looked askance at the arrangement, her defensiveness rose up. "Piper was a good kid. She never caused trouble, always did her homework. Plus, she could cook."

"A thirteen-year-old taking care of a five-year-old. You didn't resent it?"

Her automatic answer was always no. For some reason—the way Stuart looked to be reading her mind maybe—the answer died in favor of the truth. "Sometimes, but I didn't have a choice. She was family. I had a responsibility."

From behind his coffee cup, she saw Stuart give a small nod and realized if anyone understood the importance of family responsibility, he would. After all, wasn't his devotion to Ana the spark that had led to this conversation?

She continued. "When my mom died, Piper and I were left alone. I promised her we would stay together no matter what."

"And that's why you needed the money? For Piper?"

"Yeah." She stared into her cup, unsure how to continue. Talking about Piper was the easy part. It wasn't until after their mom died that the story turned bad. "My mom left us broke. Worse than broke. Actually. I didn't know what else to do."

"What about assistance? There are programs…"

"You don't understand. It wasn't that easy." How could he? Man like him, who never wanted for anything.

"But surely—"

"We were living in our car!" She hurled the answer across the table, the first time she'd ever acknowledged what happened aloud. "We were afraid if we told anyone, Piper would end up in child services, and I swore that wouldn't happen." In her mind, she saw her sister's frightened face, heard the desperation in her voice. She squeezed her eyes shut, but the memories stayed all the same. "I couldn't break my promise to her. We were all each other had. Losing her would have been like…like…"

"Losing your own child."

"Yes." His answer gave her hope that he understood. Opening her eyes, she stared across the table, silently pleading her case. "I would have done anything to keep her safe. Anything."

This was the place in the story where she should stop. Having justified her actions, there was no reason to share any more. The problem was that talking about the past was like cracking a glass. Once begun, the crack didn't stop spreading until it reached its natural end. And so the words continue to flow. "There was this guy who lived near us. Named Ben. He was always hitting on me, telling me how hot I was. Used to tell me a girl built like me could rake it in at the club where he worked. I always ignored him. Until I didn't have a choice anymore."

Unable to sit still any longer, Patience pushed herself away from the table and crossed to the back window. Her distorted reflection stared back at her in the glass. "It was January. We hadn't eaten all day. I'd lost my job—we didn't have money. Piper had a cold. Sounds like one of those over-the-top TV movies, doesn't it?" she said with a hollow laugh.

"Go on."

"I didn't know what else to do," she whispered. The desperation and shame she'd felt that fateful day returned as fresh as ever, rising up to choke the air from her lungs. "I told myself it was only for a little while. Until Piper and I were on our feet." The delusion of youth and hopelessness.

"How long did that take?"

Why was he asking? He could guess the answer. Until she went to work for Ana.

"That's the trick life plays on you," she said, resting her head against the glass. "You tell yourself it's only for a few weeks, a few months tops. Next thing you know, a few months turns into a year. Two. After a while, you start to think maybe you can't do any better. I mean, you've got no experience, so any job you can get doesn't pay nearly as much and that's assuming you could even get another job. Who's going to hire someone who danced on a table?"

"Table? Is that—?"

"Yeah. A drunk grabbed my ankle." Her breath left a smudge on the pane. Using her scarf, she wiped the mark away. If only life could clean up so easily. "Sometimes I think, if only I'd held out one more day…

"I can still feel their eyes on me," she whispered. "At night. Watching me with their dull, glassy eyes. Fantasizing about what they want to do with me." She slapped a hand against her mouth to keep from gagging as the memories began to choke her. A sob broke through anyway. "They made me feel so dirty."

"Shh." Once again Stuart was there, his face joining hers in the glass. Didn't matter that he wasn't touching her, his proximity was good enough.

"But I kept my promise," she said. "I kept us off the streets and I gave Piper a normal life." Of all the regrets she had in her life, keeping Piper safe wasn't one. "Whenever things got really bad, that's what I would tell myself. *I kept my promise.*"

Behind her, Stuart let out a long, loud breath. An echo of her own exhaustion. She hadn't expected to share so much. Telling Stuart details she'd never told anyone…the ordeal left her raw and exposed. "You said you wanted the long version."

"Yes, I did."

There was another sigh. Patience imagined him washing a hand over his features as he tried to digest everything. What would he think if he knew the one detail she'd kept back? But how could she tell him when she could barely admit the secret to herself?

"I know you think I had some big agenda, but I didn't. I ran into Ana and she confused me with a job applicant. I let her believe that's who I was and interviewed for the job." She turned so he could see she was being as honest as possible. "Ana was the first person besides Piper who ever treated me like I mattered. I swear I would never hurt her. I just needed to get out."

"You do matter," Stuart whispered.

She hated the way his words warmed her from the inside out. More so, how she couldn't help following them up with a pitiful "I do?"

"Yeah, you do." His thumb brushed her cheek, chasing away tears she didn't know had fallen. "And you deserved better."

She was too tired to argue otherwise. He'd asked for her story and she'd told him. "If you want me to leave, I will," she told him. She'd lied, and deception came with a price. Thankfully she'd squirreled away enough money so she wouldn't have to worry about living on the streets this time around. If she kept her expenses low, she'd be all right. She was a survivor.

"You don't have to leave," Stuart told her. "We all have things in our past we regret."

Tears turned her vision watery, but they were happy tears this time. "Thank you…I know I should have told the truth from the start, but I was afraid if Ana knew what I was, she would want nothing to do with me. And then, of course, you arrived, talking about how you didn't trust me and…"

"I was pretty inexorable, wasn't I?"

"If that's your way of saying you were acting like a jerk?" She was finally beginning to relax. "Then yeah."

"I'm sorry about that. You can blame Gloria."

Right. The step-grandmother. "I think I'm beginning to dislike her as much as you do."

"Trust me, that's not possible."

It was, once again, a comfortable silence wrapping around them. Patience felt lighter than she had in months—since the day she accepted the job, really. It was as if a thousand pounds had been lifted from her shoulders. Maybe, if she was lucky, the rest of her story would die a silent death, and she could enjoy that relief, as well.

"It's late," Stuart said. "You look exhausted."

She was drained. And sad, in spite of her relief. This wasn't how she'd expected the night to end. There had been magic in the air on that dance floor. For a little while she'd felt like Cinderella at the ball. But it was time to come back to reality. Having told her story, there was no way Stuart would ever look at her the same way again.

How could he? She was no longer a housekeeper; she was a housekeeper who used to take her clothes off for money.

"If it's all right with you, I think I'm going to go to bed."

"Yes, of course. I'll see you tomorrow. Good night."

"Good night." She had moved to leave when the need to say one last thing stopped her. "Thank you again for understanding." He'd probably never know how much it meant to her. On so many levels.

She expected a simple *you're welcome* in return, mainly because there didn't seem to be anything more to say. But Stuart didn't utter a word. Instead, his hand reached out to cradle her cheek. Patience's breath caught. How could a man's touch be so gentle and yet so strong? Her body yearned to lean into his hand. To close her eyes and let his strength hold her up. He swept his thumb across her cheekbone, stopping at the top of her scar. After what felt like forever, his hand dropped away. "Good night."

Patience's heart was racing so fast she was convinced it would reach her bedroom first. Twice in two nights, she'd come dangerously close to breaking the rules when it came to keeping her distance. The third time, she might not be able to walk away.

He'd wanted to know her secret. He finally did and, man, was it a doozy. Never in a million years would he have imagined Patience was… had been…he couldn't even think the word. That she'd been forced to make those kinds of choices… It made him sick to his stomach to think that in this day and age she'd felt there was no other way.

Took guts, what she'd done. And strength. Real strength. She was barely an adult and yet she'd kept her family together.

If her story was true, that is, and not some ploy for sympathy.

Immediately, he shook the distrust from his head. Damn, but he'd become such a skeptical jerk. Patience was telling the truth. He saw it in her eyes. At least he wanted to believe that's what he was seeing. He wanted to believe her as badly as he wanted to hold her. Which, he thought, washing a hand over his face, was pretty damn bad.

They were two very scary realizations.

"Nigel, why do you insist on being in the one place that makes doing my job difficult?" Patience narrowed her eyes at the cat, who, as usual, was ignoring her question. He was too busy poking at imaginary enemies in Ana's dresser drawer.

It'd been twelve long days since the dinner dance, and she was finally starting to believe that she was keeping her job. Stuart hadn't brought up the confession again. Of course, he also made himself as scarce as possible. He was on his way out the door when she woke up, and away until she went to bed. Except for that first morning when they'd recapped the dance for Ana, he'd even taken to keeping a different visiting schedule. None of his avoidance surprised her. Understanding was one thing, wanting to associate with her was another.

Back at the club, they had a saying: Prince Charming ain't walking through that door. No matter how good-looking or how amazing some guy might seem, the two of you weren't going to ride off into the sunset on his white horse. She was smart enough to know the same rule applied to housekeepers and their bosses. Say she and Stuart had slept together that night. It wouldn't have been anything more than a short-term fling, right? Being help with benefits wasn't her style.

What self-respect she had, she'd like to keep, thank you very much.

So Stuart avoiding her was a good thing. Honestly.

"Will you quit it?" She found a way out of her thoughts in time to catch Nigel snagging the lace on a pair of Ana's undergarments. "I'm pretty sure Ana wants her clothes unmolested," she said. The cat pawed at the air as she took the panties away and refolded them. Feeling bad that she'd disturbed his fun, Patience scratched behind his ear. She had a feeling part of Nigel's more-than-usual peskiness was because he missed Ana. Their promise to bring him for visits, it turned out, had been a bad idea. Nigel treated the rehab facility as he did the brownstone and wandered at will. It had taken her almost an hour to find out what room he had moved into for naptime.

"Ana will be home in another few days. In the meantime, how about you give me ten more minutes, and then we'll have a good long petting session."

As usual, Nigel wasn't interested in bargaining.

He wanted his attention and he wanted it now. Somehow he managed to wedge his head and paws into the drawer opening, and began chewing on something.

Patience rolled her eyes. "What are you doing now? Please tell me you're not trying to eat Ana's underwear." She opened the drawer and saw that the cat had found a box and was attempting to bite the corner of the cover. Her sorting and taking things the past few days must have unearthed it from the bottom of the drawer.

"You really do want to eat everything in sight, don't you?" Lifting them both free, she plopped Nigel on the bed before placing the box on the bureau. As soon as she was finished, she'd put the box back safely at the bottom of the drawer.

A knock sounded behind her. "Somehow I didn't picture you as a granny panties kind of girl," Stuart said. The sound of his voice made her stomach tumble. Swallowing back the reaction, she glanced over her shoulder. "I'm putting away Ana's laundry and packing some new items. You know, for a woman with expensive tastes, she has the most disorganized drawers I've ever seen."

It didn't skip Patience's notice that only a week before, he would have questioned what she was doing rather than make a joke. While she was touched by the show of trust, she sort of missed the protection her defensiveness gave her. When he was nice, it made keeping her distance that much harder.

"Surprised to see you here so early," she said. Here at all, really.

"We closed shop early for the holiday, and since Ana takes her post Physical Therapy nap around this time, I figured I'd work at home."

"That's right, tomorrow's Fourth of July." With all the coming and going, she'd forgotten the date. "Ana told me once how she usually has a barbecue on the roof deck."

"Barbecue in the sense that she has a caterer bring in barbecued chicken," Stuart replied. "She and her humane society buddies have been doing it for years."

"She must be devastated to have to cancel."

"Not as much as you'd think. Last I heard, Ethyl was moving the event to the rehab hospital."

Patience envisioned Ana, Ethyl and the others invading the rehab terrace with their catered dinner and cocktails. "Maybe I should be devastated on behalf of the hospital."

"Don't be. I'm sure there's a donation involved." He sat down on the edge of the bed. It was the longest and closest they'd been together since the dance. Patience studied the hands clasped between his legs. All too clear was the memory of those hands holding her close. Fingers burning a hole in the fabric of her dress. She turned back to the underwear drawer.

"Sorry I haven't been around much lately. Work has been slamming," he said.

Even the weekends? "You don't have to explain your schedule to me." Or make excuses, for that matter.

"I know, but..." The mattress made a settling noise, and she imagined him shrugging. "But I didn't want you to think that after the other night, I was...well, you know."

"Yeah." She knew. She wasn't sure she believed him, but she knew.

"Anyway, I was wondering what you were doing tomorrow."

Patience's stomach dropped. He was going to tell her he was hosting some kind of event himself, wasn't he? If she wanted a distance reminder, being asked to wait on his friends would certainly fit the bill. "It's a normal paid day off," she told him, "but if you are planning something..."

"Actually, I was wondering if you would mind checking out a condominium with me."

"What?"

"You know the new luxury tower they built near the Leather District? One of our clients is the developer. Sounds like a pretty awesome property."

"I'm sure it is." Weren't most million-dollar properties? Patience tried to ignore the pang in her chest. From the very start, Stuart had said this living arrangement was temporary. Now that Ana was close to being discharged, there was no reason for him not to look for a place of his own. What did the decision have to do with her, though?

"I was hoping you'd check out the property with me. Give me your opinion."

"The housekeeper's point of view?"

He grinned. "I was thinking more of a female point of view, but if you want to weigh in on how difficult the place will be to keep clean, feel free. Don't feel like you have to though. I know it's your day off, but if you do say yes, I'd make it worth your while."

"Worth my while, eh?" Talk about loaded language. She shivered at the potential prospects. "How?"

"I will personally show you the best seat in all of Boston for watching the fireworks."

Patience chewed the inside of her mouth. Goodness, but it was impossible to say no. Especially when the idea of sitting with him beneath the stars was so seductive.

"Sure." There'd be plenty of time to kick herself for the decision later. "What time?"

"After lunch. I figured we'd go see Ana, then meet up with Nikko. He's the developer."

"It's a—plan." She almost slipped and called it a date. Luckily she caught herself at the last moment.

What she should have been trying to catch was Nigel. Tired of being ignored, he leaped from the bed to the bureau. Problem was, he miscalculated the distance. His front paws connected with the box she'd set on the bureau, flipping it end over end. Off flew the cover, sending the contents flying.

"Bad kitty," she said. The admonishment was useless since Nigel had already bolted from the room in embarrassment.

"Here, let me help you." Stuart crouched by her on the floor, his unique Stuart scent filling the space between them. Patience had to struggle not to close her eyes and inhale. "The box was in Ana's drawer," she explained. "Nigel started chewing the cover so I moved it to the bureau." To keep it out of his reach. So much for that idea.

"Looks like a bunch of photographs."

Mementos was more like it. Patience spied newspaper clippings, tickets, playbills, what looked like drawings scribbled on napkins. Piper had kept a similar box when she was a kid.

She picked up one of the newspaper clippings. The article was written in a foreign language.

"French," Stuart said when she showed him.

"Don't suppose you can read it?"

"Sorry. Russian."

And she'd barely made it through Spanish. "This is where we need Piper."

The date said it was from the early fifties. Ana would have been just out of high school. Patience couldn't help wondering what had made her hold on to the article. The photo accompanying the article featured a trio of men standing together in front of a painting. Nothing very exciting. She was about to put the clipping in the box when one of the names jumped from the page.

"Stuart, look." She pointed to the caption. "One of the men is named Nigel Rougeau. Think it's a coincidence?"

"I don't know. The name Nigel had to come from somewhere." He slipped the clipping from her fingers and studied it closer. Like a lawyer examining evidence, Patience thought. "Looks like this was taken at some kind of art show. The wall is lined with paintings."

"But which one is Nigel?"

"Well, I can't say for sure, but based on the names listed in the caption, I'd say the one in the middle." He pointed to the bearded man with intense, dark eyes. "In fact..." He picked up one of the scattered photographs. "Here he is."

Sure enough, it was the same bearded man, only this time he was leaning against a motorbike. There were other photos, too. Nigel on the beach. In a café. One showed him standing in what looked to be an artist's studio, looking very serious and artistic as he dabbed paint on a canvas. Whoever he was, he'd obviously played a very important role in Ana's life. Important and personal.

"We should put these away," she said. It didn't feel right, poking through Ana's past. "This is obviously something very private or she wouldn't have stashed the box in her underwear drawer."

"You're right. This is none of our business." One of the pictures had fluttered a few feet away. Leaning forward, Stuart picked it up and was about to add it to the box when he froze. "Well, I'll be," he muttered.

"What?" Patience looked over his shoulder. It was another studio photo, not very different from the other one, except for maybe a few additional paintings on the wall.

"Check out the painting to the left of the easel."

It was nude portrait. A large one featuring a woman sprawled on a sofa. She was smiling at the artist, as if they shared a secret. Even in the background of a snapshot she could feel the intimacy. But why did Stuart want her to look?

"Don't you recognize the face. The smile?"

Patience studied it closer. "No way…" The smile was the same one that had greeted her the day she took the job. "Ana modeled for him?"

"More than modeled, I'd say. Which," he said,

dropping the photograph into the box, "has me feeling extra slimy for poking around."

"Yeah, definitely." Looked like Ana had her own secrets. Patience could respect that.

With the items collected, she reached for the box cover only to have Stuart reach at the same time. Their hands collided, his fingers skimming the tops of hers. Patience stilled. It was but a whisper of a touch, but it brought her skin to life with a tingling sensation that enveloped her entire body.

For most of her adult life, Patience had avoided physical contact. Look, don't touch. That was the rule. But with Stuart, even the lightest of touches had her craving more. She longed for him to take her hand. Pull her into his arms and hold her like he had the night of the dance.

She needed to back away before she lost her head. One look at Stuart's eyes said he was fighting the same battle.

"I'd better put this away before the contents spill again," she said, her voice a whisper.

"Good idea."

They stayed put, each waiting for the other to move.

"I—"

"Yeah," Stuart completed for her. He pushed himself to his feet, then offered a hand to help her up. Patience declined. Better she stand on her own two feet.

"I'll let you know what time we're going to meet Nikko tomorrow."

Who? The condominium. How could she forget. "I'll be here," she told him.

Stuart looked about to say something, only to think better of it. With one last look, he turned and left the room.

She didn't realize how badly she wanted him to stay until his footsteps had faded away.

CHAPTER SEVEN

"WE APPRECIATE YOU opening the office for us on a holiday, Nikko. I hope we didn't screw up your plans."

"Are you kidding? My wife's got her sisters at the beach house for the weekend. I'd rather do this than deal with holiday traffic any day."

Stuart and Patience shared a smile as the realtor herded them onto the elevator. While Nikko chose the floor, Stuart made a point of positioning himself in the middle. It was no secret that his client had a roving eye. The man had already stolen a glance at Patience's behind. Stuart wasn't going to let him steal another.

From the start, it had bothered him to see men checking her out. Knowing her secret, however, added a layer of protectiveness. He felt compelled to keep her from being objectified. Especially by men like Nikko Popolous.

Okay, perhaps he was doubly compelled to protect her from Nikko, whose silver hair and good looks had half the women at the firm sighing with longing.

For her part, Patience dressed in her usual nondescript style. Flowing sleeveless top and cropped jeans. He wished he knew a way to tell her that disguising her figure wasn't working. It wasn't her figure that turned men's heads—it was the whole package.

He ran his thumb across his fingertips remembering how close he'd come to kissing her yesterday. Clearly a dozen days of keeping his distance had done nothing to kill his attraction. Like that was a surprise.

But wouldn't acting on his desire make him no better than Karl Tischel and the other creeps? Worse actually, since a week ago he'd been telling her he didn't trust her. She deserved more respect than that.

"This is one of our prime corner units," Nikko

was saying as he unlocked the door. "The natural lighting is out of this world."

Patience let out a small gasp as they stepped inside. "This place is amazing!" A poker-faced negotiator, she was not.

She was right, though. The condo was nice. Hardwood floors, tons of windows.

"The open floor plan makes this a great place for entertaining," Nikko told them.

Stuart was more entertained by the sparkle in Patience's eyes as she ran a hand across the top of the kitchen island. "Everything is so clean and new."

"Top-of-the-line, too," Nikko told her. "The cabinets are solid cherry."

"There's a double oven! And a wine cooler." She smiled at Stuart. "Piper would go crazy if she saw this place."

"You need to check out the terrace. Wraps around the whole unit. Gives you another two hundred square feet. And the best part is, you don't have to share with the other tenants." The realtor slid open one of the window panels and stepped outside. "Check out this view," he said to Patience.

Stuart guided Patience out into the hot, humid air, resisting the urge to place his hand against the small of her back. The way her shirt fluttered when she walked suggested the material was light and thin. If he touched her back, he'd feel straight through to her skin and that would open up far too many problems.

"Great view, huh?"

It was nice; you could see Boston Common in the distance.

"Bet it's great at night," Patience remarked.

"Oh, at night it's spectacular," Nikko said. "There's another door that leads out here from the master bedroom. You think the kitchen was a nice setup, wait till you see the bathroom. My own bathroom isn't this fancy."

The sales patter continued while Nikko led him back into the condo and down the hall. Stuart didn't listen. A sales pitch was a sales pitch. All he wanted was a place to sleep that accrued a good return on investment.

Damn, but he'd grown jaded.

Once upon a time, he might have hunted for a home instead of an investment. When he was younger. Someplace like what he remembered sharing with his parents.

Of course, maybe things would be different if he were condo shopping with someone. Someone whose eyes sparkled with excitement.

The bathroom was impressive. Designer vanities, giant sunken tub in thecorner. "Beat's Ana's claw-foot tub, doesn't it?" he said to Patience.

There was no answer.

"I think she stayed on the terrace," Nikko remarked.

Indeed, when Stuart stepped through the bedroom slider, he found her in the same place as before, her attention fixed on some faraway point.

He had to stop and grab the railing as desire rolled through him. Why was keeping his distance a bad idea again?

It wasn't until he walked closer that he saw the sadness behind the faraway gaze. "Everything all right?"

"Great," she replied. "Why wouldn't it be?"

He settled in next to her. "You tell me. You looked a million miles away."

"I was thinking how you could fit my old apartment into this place's living room."

"It's the lack of furniture. Makes the space seem bigger."

"No, our apartment was that small."

There was regret in her voice that didn't belong. "Bet it was easy to clean," he teased.

He got the smile he was hoping for. "Didn't take long, for sure."

Nor, Stuart bet, did the apartment ever feel empty and cold. "And, you had your sister."

"True. I'd pick small over losing her in a second, even if she did take over the bathroom when she hit high school. There was only one electrical plug that could handle a blow-dryer," she said when he chuckled. "For four years, I was lucky to get my hair dried in time for work."

Patience would never believe him, but he envied her. Her closeness with her sister, that is. Despite everything the two of them had endured, they'd always had each other to cling to. He wished he had that kind of support. Sure, he had Ana, but their closeness hadn't really developed until he came east for law school. Before that…well, no wonder Gloria was able to charm him blind.

Looking to the ground, he concentrated on plowing little piles of grit and dirt with his shoe. "My grandfather's house was big," after a moment. "It actually had wings."

"You mean like in west wing, east wing—that sort of thing?"

"Uh-huh." Though his attention remained on the ground, he imagined her eyes widening. "There were literally days when I wouldn't see Grandpa Theodore even though we were in the same house."

"Not at all?"

"Not unless I went looking for him." Attempts that were met with varying degrees of success.

"I'm sorry."

No, he didn't want her sympathy any more than she did. "He was…busy," he said too, to steal her word.

Patience slid her hand to the left until their fingers aligned, her little finger flush with his. "I understand."

Yeah, she did, thought Stuart, but then he'd known as much for a while. Same way he knew that as lonely as his teenage years had been, they were a cakewalk compared to hers.

He itched to cover her hand with his and entwine their fingers. Would she pull away if he did?

"The view is irresistible, isn't it?" Nikko stepped onto the terrace, making the decision for him. The realtor waved his phone. "Sorry. My wife couldn't find the air pump. Don't know why—the thing's right in the center of the garage."

"Are you telling this guy he needs to buy?" Nikko asked Patience.

She laughed. "I think that's up to him."

"Maybe, but I did bring you here for input. What do you think?"

"I think this is the most amazing apartment I've ever seen outside of Ana's brownstone."

"Those brownstones are great, but they come with their headaches. Like parking. Brownstones don't come with parking," Nikko said. "And did you see the cedar closet in the laundry area? Solid cedar, not veneer. A moth would need a drill to get at your winter wardrobe. To put something like that in custom would cost you a fortune."

As opposed to spending a fortune on a condominium that already had one. Stuart was about to reply when he realized Nikko had been directing his remarks to Patience. He was assuming it would be her wardrobe hanging in the cedar closet.

Patience, staying here. The idea didn't strike him nearly as improbable as it should. On the contrary, the longing from earlier reared again, tendrils spreading up and across his chest. He hadn't realized until just now that when he left Ana's brownstone, he would be leaving Patience behind. Strange as it seemed, he'd grown used to sharing a space with her. He would miss her presence. That's what the ache in his chest was all about. He was going to miss having company.

* * *

"All I'm saying is that most people would have at least slept on the decision," Patience said when they got back to the brownstone.

"I don't know why you're so surprised. You said yourself the place was amazing."

"It is. But I didn't mean for you to whip out your checkbook and write a down payment." Last thing she wanted was the responsibility of having influenced his decision. Picking up Nigel's dish, she headed to the cupboard. "How do you know there isn't someplace better out there?" she asked, pulling out a can of Salmon Delight.

"There might be, and if I were looking for the perfect apartment, that would be important, but I'm not. This place is close to my office, and a good investment. I had pretty much made up my mind to buy if the space was halfway decent."

If that was so, why invite her?

"I really did want a second opinion," he replied when she asked. "If both of us liked the space, then I knew the condo was a winner."

"Oh, sure, because I've so much experience

buying luxury property. You do realize when I said it was the most amazing place outside of the brownstone that it was also the only other high-end place I've ever looked at."

"You sell yourself short. You zoned right in on the areas I wanted an opinion on. The laundry room, the kitchen, the living space."

All the cleaning woman areas of expertise. She winced and tried to take the compliment the way he meant. "The kitchen was nice."

"So I could tell by the way your eyes lit up." Okay, now she was blushing. He was studying her eyes?

"Here I thought I was being so calm and sophisticated."

"You were being yourself, which—before you make a comment—is exactly what I wanted. You'll argue otherwise, but you're not very good when it comes to hiding your thoughts."

"I'm not?" Impossible. She'd spent years cultivating her stone face. She knew how to block out the audience with the best of them.

However, she had been off her game since Stuart moved in. Did that mean he knew how badly she'd been struggling to keep her attraction at arm's length?

Luckily, Stuart couldn't see her face or he'd really be able to read her feelings. The overheated cheeks were a dead giveaway.

"How else do you think I figured out you were keeping secrets? Your eyes gave you away. They always do," he said. "I see it all the time in depositions. Body language is a killer. Although in this case…you weren't exactly hiding your enthusiasm."

"I did gush a little, didn't I?"

"A little?" Patience didn't have to be a body language expert to read the amusement on his face.

"Okay, a lot," she conceded. "That didn't mean you had to buy the place. I don't think I could be that impulsive." She had trouble buying anything on a whim. What if you needed the cash later on?

"I told you, I had already decided—"

"Before we got there. I know what you said,

but this afternoon was still the first time you saw the place. That, to me, is impulsive. How do you know you got the best place?"

He shrugged. "It's just a condominum."

"Just?" His comment made it sound as if he was settling, and while Patience wasn't expecting him to gush about the place like her, she had expected him to at least care about where he lived.

"I work seventy to eighty hours a week," he explained. "I'm hardly ever home. As long as the place is close to my office and can fit a bed, that's all I care about."

So he was settling. Patience wasn't sure what saddened her more: that or how little he had in his life. Something Karl Tischel said at the dinner dance popped into her head. *The one whose girlfriend dumped him.* Was work the reason? Or did he work because he'd been dumped? Either way, his life sounded lonely. Correction. He sounded lonely, Patience realized.

Apparently, she wasn't the only one who couldn't hide her emotions.

Even so, she shouldn't want to reach out and

comfort him the way she did. Certainly not after watching him spend a million dollars without blinking an eye. What more proof did she need that they were from different worlds?

And yet his loneliness spoke to a place deep inside her, making her feel closer to him than ever.

"What's with the take-out bag?" In Stuart's hand was a large white paper bag with handles. On the way home, he'd insisted they stop at the local market. He made her wait outside while he went in, only to return a few minutes later with a bag of food. Patience had been curious then, and she was doubly curious now. She leaped on the topic as the perfect change of conversation.

"Dinner," he replied. "I seem to recall promising you a picnic and fireworks."

"Yes, you did. The best seats in Boston, you said."

"Trust me, they are."

Nigel sauntered into the kitchen and crouched by his empty food dish, waiting for Patience to fill it. The minute Patience crossed his path, he began weaving around and between her legs. "You're lucky we aren't on the stairs," she told him.

"Don't you mean *you're* lucky?" Stuart replied. "As far as I can tell, Nigel isn't the one who gets hurt."

"True." Patience thought of the photographs they'd found yesterday. Ana had once said Nigel had a "Nigel personality." If the original was as pesky as his namesake, that might explain why he wasn't around anymore.

Behind her, Stuart was unpacking the tote bag. She saw containers loaded with potato salad, fried chicken, fruit and chocolate cake—enough to feed a full army. "So where is this awesome picnic spot?" she asked. "Near the Boston Esplanade?"

"Nope. The roof."

"Ana's roof?"

"Sure. That's why the humane society insists she throw the summer barbeques here. You won't find a better view, not even on the Esplanade."

He pointed to the utility closet in the corner

of the kitchen. "Is the portable radio still on the shelf?"

"I think so."

"Great. Grab it and a couple of glasses, will you? I'll go set up the table."

The rooftop deck had been something of a marvel to Patience. Before her accident, Ana had ocassionally taken afternoon tea up there. In Patience's old neighborhood, a deck meant a place to keep a couple plastic chairs or small table for eating outside, but Ana's deck was an outside living room. No plastic chairs or cheap furniture here. Instead, there was a love seat and matching chairs. Floor lamps, too. Four of them, one in each corner so as to light the entire space once the sun went down. Potted evergreens and other plants brought nature into the arrangement while a pair of heaters added warmth in the colder weather.

One of her first major housekeeping projects had been to bring the cushions indoors and cover the furniture. Then, as she did now, she found herself in awe that such a beautiful room could exist outdoors.

It was a perfect summer night, made for sitting under the stars. A three-quarter moon hung high and yellow in the cloudless sky. Before them a mosaic of rooftops and lights spread as far as the eye could see. The beacon atop old John Hancock Tower glowed blue, telegraphing the beautiful weather to anyone who needed reminding.

Stuart was opening a bottle of wine when she arrived. "You don't mind, do you?" he asked her. "If you'd rather, there's water..."

"No, wine would be great." Even if it did make the atmosphere feel more date-like. "After all, it's a holiday right?"

"Right. What's Independence Day without a toast to freedom?"

Walking over to the edge of the deck, Patience looked out across the city. "I can see your apartment building from here, I think. Over there." She pointed to a tower in the distance. "I can't remember if I could see Ana's roof from the terrace or not."

"We'll have to stand outside and wave to each other someday to find out." He appeared at her elbow, carrying a glass of wine in each hand. Handing her one, he raised the other. "To freedom."

Patience gave a slight smile as she raised hers in return. "One of us achieved freedom today. How long before you move?"

"The end of the month, I think. I want to make sure Ana's mobile enough before I go, so as to not put all the burden on you."

"That's sweet of you."

"I want to." Perhaps, but Patience didn't harbor any illusions. He was looking out for Ana because he loved his aunt, not her.

Not that love had anything to do with anything.

"Did I say something wrong?"

And here she thought staring at her glass would keep her eyes from giving her away. "Just thinking a month wasn't that far away. Ana will be sorry to see you go."

"Ana?" He moved in tighter, giving her little choice but to turn and meet his gaze. Questions hung in the back of their blue depths. He knew she meant both her and Ana, but she couldn't bring herself to admit it.

"Don't be silly. You know she adores you. It has to be killing her to be in the hospital while you're here in the brownstone."

"It's killing me," he replied. "Seeing her laid up reminds me of how old she's getting. And how frail."

"Part of me wants to think she'll be here forever," he added, contemplating the contents of his glass.

Patience could feel the regret pressing down on his shoulders and rushed to reassure him. "We always want to think that the people we love will stay forever. I'm as guilty as you are. I want to believe Piper will be part of my world forever, but someday she's going to have a life of her own. It's already started."

"You make it sound like she'll forget you exist."

"Forget no, but she'll have other priorities beyond her big sister." The way it was supposed to be. She hadn't sacrificed in order for Piper to stay by her side.

"Maybe you'll be too busy having a life of your own to notice."

Doing what? Cleaning? "Oh, I'll have a life, but I want more for Piper. I want her to have everything. Love, family, a home."

"Who says you won't have those things, too?"

She'd love to have them, but they seemed too far out of reach. Easier to wish happiness for Piper. "Maybe someday," she said, speaking into her wine. "At the moment, I'm happy where I am. Working for Ana."

"You know you deserve more, right?" His fingers caught her chin and turned her face toward him. "Right?" he repeated.

Patience wanted to tell him to stop being so kind. Things were easier when he'd been suspicious. At least then she knew the dividing line. Attraction bad, distance good. When he was sweet and tender like this, the line blurred. She could feel the cracks in her invisible wall growing bigger. Pretty soon there would be no wall at all to protect her.

But she couldn't tell him any of that—not without admitting his growing hold over her. "Maybe someday," she repeated with a smile. Stepping away from his touch, she looked to the Esplanade, the long expanse of green lining the Charles River. "You're right, this is the best picnic spot. You can see the Hatch Shell," she said, jumping once again to a safe topic. The area around the open-air stage glowed white from all the spotlights and television trucks. "I swear I can hear the music."

"I'm not surprised. We're close enough." Behind her, Patience heard shuffling, and suddenly the music grew louder. He'd turned on the radio simulcast. "There," she heard him say, "that's better than straining to catch a stray chord. Sounds like the concert just started. Plenty of time before the fireworks."

"Do you know," Patience said, stepping away from the view, "that I've never seen the July Fourth fireworks live?"

"Really?"

"Nope. Just on TV. Piper was afraid of loud noises so I never took her. We stayed home and watched them on TV instead."

"How about when you were a kid? Sorry." He seemed to realize his mistake as soon as he spoke.

"That's all right. There are worse things to miss out on." She took a plate and started helping herself to the food. "How about you? What did your family do on Fourth of July?"

"Nothing. I was at camp, learning important wilderness survival techniques, like how not to lose your inhaler while hiking."

She laughed.

"I'm not kidding," he said. "I lost that sucker twice one summer. Kept falling out of my pocket."

"I'm sorry," Patience said, "but I'm having a hard time picturing you as this awkward asthmatic."

"Remind me to show you my high school graduation photo someday. You'll believe me then."

"Well, you're definitely not awkward now."

"Thank you." Stuart's smile had an odd cast to it, almost as if he didn't quite believe her. Which was ridiculous, because surely he knew what kind of man he was, didn't he?

They ate in silence, letting the music fill in for conversation. It never failed to surprise Patience how comfortable just being with Stuart could be. Simmering attraction aside, that is. Maybe it was more that she never felt uncomfortable with him. Never felt like he was trying to mentally undress her. Even those moments of intense scrutiny, when his eyes bore down on her, weren't about her figure, but rather what was inside. With him, Patience never felt like less than a person.

It was a gift she'd never forget.

Feeling a lump begin to rise in her throat, she reached for her wine. This wasn't the time for tears.

"How do you think Ana's party is going? She seemed pretty excited when we saw her this morning."

"Going great, I'm sure." Stuart smiled while wiping the grease from his fingers. "No doubt she and her cronies have commandeered the entire hospital sunroom and put the staff to work. Those ladies can be a force to be reckoned with. Don't be surprised if we show up tomorrow and hear they had the whole hospital involved."

Patience could picture the scene. "They'll miss her when she's discharged." She sipped her wine thoughtfully. "I'm surprised you're not at a party yourself."

"I promised you a picnic for viewing the condo with me."

"We could have done it a different night." He must have had better options than spending the night with her.

"No, I said I'd show you the best place to see the fireworks. Besides, I wanted to."

Patience tried not to get too excited by the remark. Unfortunately, she failed. The idea that Stuart had chosen her warmed her to the core. "I hope your friends aren't too disappointed."

"They'll survive, I'm sure." He stared at his drink, looking as if he was debating saying more.

"I don't—I don't have a lot of friends. At least not close ones."

"I'm surprised."

He looked up. "Are you? In case you haven't noticed, I tend to be rather suspicious of people."

Because of Gloria? Wow, his step-grandmother had really done a number on him. Or was there someone else who'd hurt him, too? The woman who "dumped him" maybe?

"Dr. Tischel told me about your ex-girlfriend," she told him.

"What did he say?"

She was right—the way his spine straightened told her that his step-grandmother hadn't been the only woman to burn his trust. "Not much. Only that she broke up with you."

"He didn't say anything else?"

Like what? Seeing Stuart on alert had her curious. "No. He didn't even mention her name." The fact he'd brought up the subject at all had made Patience think she wasn't just any girlfriend but rather someone who had broken his heart.

Stuart's reaction all but confirmed her theory.

Waving away the comment with exaggerated indifference, he sat back in his seat. "Dr. Tischel was drunk and looking to spread gossip is all."

Patience wasn't so sure. Dr. Tischel had spoken pretty offhandedly for a guy trying to gossip. In fact, he sounded more as if he was repeating news everyone already knew.

She was about to ask for Stuart's version when he held up his hand. "Listen," he said. The orchestra was playing a medley of Big Band songs. Memories of swaying in each other's arms came rushing back, the onslaught overwhelming all other thoughts. One look at Stuart's darkening eyes told her he remembered, too.

"Let's dance," he said, setting down his glass. It wasn't a request but a command. The assertiveness sent a thrill running down her spine. Her hand was in his before she could think twice.

"What are the odds?" she heard him murmur as he pulled her close.

"I don't know." And she didn't care. She would dance to anything if it meant being able to spend time in his arms. You are such a goner, she thought as she rested her temple against his shoulder.

"This is the first time I've ever danced without mile-high heels," she said. "I feel short."

His chest rumbled beneath her ear. "You could always stand on tiptoes."

"That's okay, this is perfect." More than perfect. Closing her eyes, she let the moment wash over her. Who knew when they'd share another one? "Much better than the dinner dance."

Stuart pulled back and his eyes searched hers. "You mean that, don't you?"

There was something about his voice. In a way he sounded surprised, but a bigger part of him sounded pleased, as if he'd made a great discovery.

"You still don't trust me to tell you the truth, do you?" After everything she'd shared about her past...

"That's just it, I do," he said, pulling her close again. "For the first time in a long time, I do."

They swayed in silence. Patience lost herself in the music and the sound of Stuart's breathing as they turned around and around, their feet and their bodies in perfect sync. The roof, the streets below, the entire city—all fell away except for the two of them.

The song ended, replaced by the slow mournful strands of the "1812 Overture," Boston's signal the fireworks were on their way. Patience clung tighter, wishing the moment would never end.

"Gloria," Stuart whispered suddenly. The name made Patience's insides chill.

"The girlfriend who broke up with me. It was Gloria."

CHAPTER EIGHT

DEAR GOD. WAS he saying…? "You had an affair with your step-grandmother?" It was a lousy question, but she had to ask. Gloria was, after all, married to a man sixty years her senior. It would be only natural that she might turn to someone young and virile.

Besides, the alternative would be that Gloria chose Theodore over…

"No affair."

Her stomach sank. Exactly what she'd feared. "She left you for your grandfather." The *ew* factor increased. What kind of woman would prefer an old man to…to Stuart?

She already knew the answer. "She was after the money."

"Yeah." He broke away. Patience tried to grab his hand to pull him back only to miss the mark.

"I should have realized. I mean, she pursued me—that alone should have been my first clue."

"Why?" Patience didn't understand. She pictured women coming on to Stuart all the time.

He laughed at her question. A soft, sad laugh. "Asthmatic and awkward, remember? Well, awkward anyway. This was almost fifteen years ago," he rushed to add. He must have guessed she was about to argue the point. "I hadn't grown into myself yet. When it came to things like dating, I was pretty clueless. Gloria on the other hand…let's say she'd grown into herself years earlier. When she started showing interest in me, I thought I was the luckiest guy in the world. Couldn't wait to introduce her to Grandpa Theodore. Talk about a stupid mistake."

"She started chasing after him."

"Hey, why settle for the nerdy grandson when you can snag the mother lode, right?" The bitterness in his voice told the rest of the story. Along with his eyes. He could try to make a joke out of the betrayal, but she could still feel his hurt. As he'd said before, the eyes gave away everything.

Having told his story, or as much as he intended, he made his way back to the coffee table. "Although to be fair, Grandpa Theodore did his part, too." Snagging his wineglass, he drained the contents. "In a way I'm grateful to them," he said, reaching for the bottle. He started to pour, only to change his mind, and set it back down. "They taught me a valuable lesson."

"Be careful who you trust."

"Exactly. I promised myself I would never— ever—get taken in again. Wasn't long after that I came out here and connected with Ana."

Who became the one relative he could trust. Patience understood now why he'd been so suspicious of her when they'd met. Like her, Stuart had built himself an invisible wall. Granted, he'd built his for different reasons, but the purpose was the same: self-defense. So long as he kept the world at a distance, he would be safe.

He'd shared his history with her, though. To think he'd allowed her to see a part of him few people ever saw. Tears sprang to her eyes, she was so honored. What little there was left of the walls protecting Patience's heart crumbled to dust.

It was a mistake. Every bit of her common sense knew better. A woman like her, a man like him. Temporary, at best. But she couldn't help herself. The need for distance forgotten, she brushed her fingers along his jaw.

"Gloria was a fool," she whispered, hoping he could read in her eyes the words she wasn't saying.

"Are you sure?" Stuart whispered back. He wasn't asking about Gloria, but about her. Was she sure she wanted to cross the line they were toeing.

The answer was no, but surety had long since fallen by the wayside in favor of emotion. Patience melted into his arms as his lips found hers.

In the distance, fireworks exploded over the Charles River. Neither noticed.

The first thing Patience noticed in the morning was the pressure bearing down on her chest. She opened her eyes to discover Stuart lying next to her, his arm flung possessively across her body. Remembering the night before, she smiled. Funny, but she expected the morning after to be uncomfortable, with regrets darkening the light of day, but no. She was so happy she felt as if her chest might explode.

Her smile widened as Stuart gave a soft moan and moved in closer. "Morning," he murmured. With his voice laced with sleep, he sounded young and unjaded.

Blue eyes blinked at her. "I see you."

"I see you, too."

"No, I mean I can see you. I fell asleep wearing my contacts again."

"Again, huh? Happens often?"

"More than I want to admit." He rolled to his side. "In this case, though, I blame you."

"Me?" she asked, rolling to face him.

"Uh-huh. You distracted me."

"Oh." She was going to strain her cheek muscles if she kept smiling this way. "I didn't hear any complaints last night."

"Oh, trust me, there are no complaints this morning, either."

They lay side by side, his arm draped around her waist. The intimate position felt so natural it was scary. "But I better not hear any jokes about my glasses."

"I like your glasses. They give you a sexy hipster look."

Stuart laughed. It was a sound everyone should hear in the morning. "Maybe we should get you some glasses." His smile shifted, turning almost reverent. "You really mean what you're saying, though, don't you?"

"Doesn't make a different to me whether you wear glasses or not. You could wear a sack over your head for all I care. Well, maybe not a sack. I kind of like your face."

"I like yours," he said, brushing her cheek. Her face. Not her body. Patience loved the way he looked at her. He didn't see her as an object or even as an ex-stripper. As far as Stuart was concerned, she was a person. Someone worthy of respect.

But do you deserve it? The question came crashing into her brain, reminding her that, in spite of all her confessions, there was still one secret she'd kept to herself. Stuart trusted her enough to tell his story. Maybe she should trust him with the rest of hers?

His fingers were moving south, tracing a path over her shoulder, tugging the sheet away from her skin.

"Stuart...?"

"Mmm?"

"I—" She arched into the sheets as he nuzzled the crook of her neck. "Nothing." He made it way too easy to give in.

Ana was talking a blue streak. "...need more events like last evening's. I asked Dr. O'Hara to get me the CEO's phone number. When I'm settled back home, I want to make a donation and tell him to earmark the money for entertainment. As I told Dr. O'Hara, patients need distractions, and he agreed. I have to say, I wasn't sure I was going to like him but he's much less condescending than Karl. Plus, he has a lovely wife, so he won't be bothering Patience. Are you listening to me?"

"Of course, I am. Dr. O'Hara's condescending."

He wasn't even close, was he? Stuart could tell from Ana's arched brow. "Sorry, I was thinking about…something else." This morning, to be exact. And last night.

"Obviously." His aunt settled back against her pillow. Time in the rehab facility had improved the sharpness of her stare, which she used to full advantage. "So what is it that has you smiling like the cat who ate the canary? It's unlike you."

"I'm in a good mood is all. I found a condo yesterday. On the other side of the Common."

"Does that mean you'll be moving out?"

"Not for a while yet."

The disappointment left Ana's face. "Good. I'm not ready for you to leave yet."

Neither was he. It had dawned on him this morning that leaving would mean leaving Patience behind. Unless they continued whatever it was they were doing at his place. Was that what he wanted?

Pictures of her standing on his terrace flashed through his head.

"You're smiling again. Must be a very nice apartment."

"It's not bad. Patience came with me to check the place out. She liked it."

"Really? I didn't realize you valued her opinion? I got the impression there was tension between the two of you."

"We…" Damn, if his cheeks weren't getting warm. "We worked that out."

"Did you, now?"

"We talked."

"I'm glad. She's a lovely girl, isn't she?"

"Um…" He pictured her face when she woke up this morning. Hair mussed. Sleep in her eyes. She was far more than lovely. She was genuine and honest. He could trust her.

The realization hit him while they were dancing. Scared the hell out of him. At the same time, he'd never felt freer.

"Stuart?"

"You were right, Tetya. She's terrific."

He could tell the second his aunt put two and two together. Her pale blue eyes pinned him to the chair. "Are you having an affair with my housekeeper?"

Stuart ran a hand across the back of his neck. His cheeks were definitely crimson now. Thankfully, his aunt took pity on him and waved her question off. "You don't have to say anything. I know a besotted look when I see one."

"I'm not sure I'd say besotted." A word from this century, perhaps.

"Use whatever word you want. I'm glad."

"You are?"

"Of course. You let what happened with Gloria keep you from falling in love for way too long. Killed me to think Theodore crushed *your* heart, too."

Who said anything about love? He was about to tell Ana she was reading too much into the affair when something his aunt said caught his attention.

"Too?" This was the first time his aunt had ever referred to the bad blood between her and his grandfather. He thought of the memory box buried at the bottom of her drawer, of cats all bearing the same man's name, and his heart ached for the woman he'd grown to love as a grandmother. What had his grandfather done? He had to ask. "Are you talking about Nigel?"

"Don't be silly? What would your grandfather have to do with my cat?"

She was a worse liar than he was. The way she suddenly became interested in smoothing her sheets gave her away. "I meant Nigel Rougeau," he said.

Her hand stilled. "Who?"

"I saw the photographs, Tetya. The ones in your drawer."

"Oh."

"I know it's none of my business…I've just always wondered why. What could my grandfather have possibly done to make you cut us off?"

"Oh, *lapushka*, I was never trying to cut you

off. What happened was a long time ago, before you were ever born."

"You mean what happened with Nigel?"

She nodded.

She didn't get to say anything further. Footsteps sounded outside the hospital door and, a second later, Patience appeared. Stuart couldn't believe the way his pulse picked up when he saw her.

"Hey," she greeted in a shy voice that screamed all the things they'd done overnight. "I was bringing Ana something to eat. I didn't realize you'd be here."

"I decided to visit during lunch so I could get home at a decent hour," he replied. His answer made her blush, probably because they both knew why he wanted to get home early. The pink ran across her cheeks and down her neck, disappearing into the collar of her T-shirt. She looked so incredibly delectable Stuart had to grip the sides of his chair to keep from kissing her senseless.

"I brought you a chicken salad sandwich," she said, setting a bag on Ana's bedside table. Then, noticing his aunt's distraction, she frowned. "Am I interrupting something?"

"Ana was about to tell me about Nigel Rougeau." That made Ana look up.

"She was the one who found the box," he explained.

"We weren't trying to pry, I swear," Patience said. "I put the box on the bureau while I was organizing your drawer and Nigel—the cat—knocked it on the floor. We saw the name when we were picking up the mess. I'm sorry."

"Don't be, dear. It was probably Nigel's way of demanding attention." Ana gave a long, sad sigh. "He never did like being kept a secret."

She meant Nigel Rougeau. Realizing this, Stuart and Patience exchanged a look. Apparently cats and their namesake shared personality traits after all.

"Maybe it's time I told our story," Ana said, smoothing the sheets again.

"Should I leave?" Patience asked. "Let you talk about family business…"

"No, dear. You can stay," Ana told her. "You're like family."

Stuart could tell Patience was still wavering, so he grabbed her hand and pulled her into the chair next to his. "Please stay."

She looked down at their joined fingers. "This is okay, too," he said. "She knows."

"Oh." The blush returned.

"Nigel loved when women blushed. He used to say every woman's cheek has its own special shade. He was a painter I knew in Paris."

"You were his model. The painting on the wall."

"He and I preferred the term *muse*. Our relationship was far deeper than artist and model." She sighed. "He had such talent."

The reverence in her voice took Stuart aback. "Why didn't you mention him before?" he asked. Why keep a man she so clearly worshipped a secret?

"Some things are too painful to mention." Next to him, Patience stiffened. They both understood all too well what Ana meant. "You don't have to tell us now, either," Patience said.

"Yes," he agreed. "We'll understand."

"No, I want to. I'm sure he's furious that I've stayed quiet this long." Ana spoke in the present tense, as if he were in the room with them.

"We met the summer I graduated high school. I was on a grand tour, being bored to tears with tours of cathedrals and palaces and had sneaked away to see some of the more forbidden parts of Paris. Instead, I met Nigel. It was love at first sight. When the tour moved on, I stayed behind."

Her voice grew gravelly. Stuart reached over and poured her a glass of water. As he handed the drink to her, he saw her eyes had grown wet. "We were going to do great things in the art world. He would paint, I would be the inspiration. The Diakonova to his Salvador Dali."

"What happened?" Patience asked. The two of them leaned forward, curious.

"Your grandfather happened, of course. You know our parents passed away when I was a child." Stuart nodded. Losing your parents young seemed to be Duchenko tradition.

"Because he was the eldest, Theodore became

my legal guardian. When he found out Nigel and I were living together—Nigel considered marriage a bourgeois institution—he went crazy. He flew to Paris to 'bring me home.' Said he would not allow his seventeen-year-old sister to ruin the Duchenko name by living in sin with some two-bit, fortune-hunting painter. I always wondered whether if Nigel had been more successful, if Theodore might have had a different view."

She paused to take another drink before continuing. "And then, he saw Nigel's work."

"The painting hanging in the studio."

His aunt gave a wistful smile. "That was one of so many studies. Nigel was a student of the human form and being his muse…"

"He studied your form the most." Patience's comment earned a blush. It was the first time Stuart ever saw his aunt color in embarrassment.

"Your grandfather was doubly furious. He told me in no uncertain terms that if I didn't come home and live like a proper lady, he would destroy Nigel's career before it had ever started."

Patience gave a soft gasp. "Surely, he didn't mean..."

"I'm sure he did," Stuart replied. "Grandpa Theodore could be ruthless when he wanted to be." Didn't matter who was involved. His sister, his grandson.

Reading his mind, Patience squeezed his hand, the gesture replacing the emptiness inside him with warmth. Grateful, he pressed her fingers to his lips.

"What did you do?" he asked Ana, knowing the answer.

"What could I do? I was only seventeen. If I refused, it would be the end of Nigel's career, and I couldn't do that to him. He was born for greatness."

So, instead, she sacrificed her happiness for his sake. Stuart wanted to strangle his grandfather.

"You must have loved him very much," Patience whispered.

"He was my soul mate." Ana smiled a watery smile, only to have it melt away seconds later. "I told Nigel, I'd come back. That as soon as I was eighteen I would find him. We could use my money to protect ourselves from Theodore's influence."

"But you didn't go back." She'd moved to Boston and never returned to Paris.

A tear slipped down Ana's face. "There was nothing to go back to. A few weeks after I left, Nigel was killed in a motorcycle accident. He always rode too fast…"

Her voice grew wobbly, and the tears fell more frequently. "Later I heard Theodore had hired someone to purchase all his paintings of me and have them destroyed. All his work gone forever."

"Oh, Tetya." There were no words. Stuart jumped to his feet and wrapped his arms around her, anger toward his grandfather building as Ana shook silently against him. Here he'd thought marrying Gloria was the old man's low point. He couldn't be more wrong.

A comforting warmth buffeted him. Patience stood by his side, her hand gently rubbing circles on Ana's back. "I'm so sorry," she whispered.

Giving a sniff, his aunt lifted her head. While

her eyes were red and puffy, Stuart saw the familiar backbone finding its way back. "My sweet child," she said, swiping at her cheeks, "why are you apologizing? You didn't do anything. Either of you."

Her absolution did little to alleviate the hurt he felt on her behalf. "But if I'd known…"

"What? You'd have called him on his behavior? Theodore knew what he was doing. He was a selfish man who didn't care who he hurt."

No, thought Stuart, he didn't.

She touched his cheek, tenderly, like the surrogate grandmother she'd become. "I'm just glad he didn't destroy your heart the way he did mine."

"Me, too." Although he'd come damn close.

Emotionally and physically worn-out, Ana dozed off a short while later. Patience waited by the doorway while Stuart tucked the older woman in and gave her a goodbye kiss.

"This explains why she named all the cats Nigel," Patience said, once they stepped into the corridor. "She was keeping her lover's memory alive." It broke her heart to think of Ana—sweet, gentle Ana—spending a lifetime mourning her only love. How could Theodore ruin his sister's happiness like that? All because she'd dared to fall in love with the wrong kind of man?

Life really did stink sometimes.

Out of the corner of her eye, she saw Stuart looking back over his shoulder. "I knew my grandfather could be cold, but I always thought what happened with Gloria was a case of him being seduced. Now I wonder…" Rather than finish the sentence, he looked down at the linoleum. Didn't matter. Patience could guess what he was thinking. In spite of what he said regarding his grandfather's involvement, he still placed the bulk of the betrayal on Gloria's shoulders. Ana's story shifted the blame more evenly. "Ironic, isn't it?" he said. "My grandfather being so intent on protecting the Duchenko name and fortune, only to make a spectacle of himself decades later by marrying a fortune hunter himself?"

"You heard Ana. He was selfish. Selfish people only care about what benefits them."

"True." He left out a deep breath. "Goes to show, you really can't trust anyone."

"That's not true." Patience rushed to keep the walls from reforming. "You can trust Ana. And you can trust me." Staring directly at him, she dared him to look into her soul and see her sincerity. "I swear."

"I know." He went back to studying the floor.

This morning, Patience had joked about his glasses looking sexy and hip. At the moment, however, he just looked lost. It felt like the most natural thing in the world to wrap her arms around her waist and hold him close. He started at first, but it wasn't long before he hugged her back, his chin resting on her shoulder. "I'm as bad as he was, you know that?"

"What are you talking about?" Pulling back, she frowned at him. "If you're talking about your grandfather, you couldn't be more wrong." The two men were day and night. "I've seen how much you care about Ana. For crying out loud, you've been in here visiting every day since the accident. You make sure she has the best doctors, the best therapy. Hell, you went to the humane society dinner dance for her."

She pressed herself tight in his arms. "You could never do what your grandfather did to Ana," she whispered in his ear. Or what his grandfather had done to him. "Not in a million years."

"You sound pretty confident."

"I am," she replied with a smile. "There's a reason Ana sings your praises so much. You're a good man, Stuart Duchenko." Her heart echoed every word.

Stuart squeezed her tight, and for a second Patience thought she felt his body shake. The moment didn't last. Slipping out of her embrace, he crossed the hall and moved to a new doorway. There he stood, staring into an unoccupied room. "My pity party must sound pretty pathetic to you."

Because, he was saying, she'd had it so much worse. Maybe so, but as she'd told him before, it wasn't a contest. "Everyone needs reassurance once in a while."

"That so?" A smile made its way to his face as he leaned against the door frame. "Well, in that case, I hope you know how awesome you are, Patience Rush. I'm damn lucky our paths crossed."

On the contrary, she was the lucky one. She was falling deeper and deeper by the second.

"Thank you for being here." Leaning forward, he kissed her. A long, lingering kiss, the tenderness of which left Patience's head spinning. "See you back home?"

Not trusting herself to speak, she nodded. If there was any chance that she could keep her heart from getting involved, that kiss chased it away for good.

CHAPTER NINE

THAT NIGHT, THE two of them lay on the deck's top sofa, legs and bodies entwined like spaghetti, making out like a pair of teenagers. Patience swore Stuart had turned kissing into an art form. One moment his kisses were possessive and demanding, the next they turned so reverent they brought tears to her eyes.

All the while Patience fought the voice in her head warning her that he'd eventually realize she wasn't good enough.

She was saved from her dark thoughts by Stuart tugging on her lower lip with his teeth. "I think I'm love with your mouth," he murmured.

Words muttered in the throes of passion, but Patience's heart jumped all the same. She forced herself to treat the remark as lightly as he intended it to be. Running her bare foot up Stuart's leg, she thrilled at the way her touch caused a soft groan. "What does *lapushka* mean?" she asked.

Stuart raised himself up on his elbows. "Seriously?"

"I'm curious." And she needed the distraction. He might have been only talking about her mouth, but the word *love* required her to take a step back. "I know *tetya* means aunt…"

"*Lapushka* means little paw. And before you ask, I have no idea why she calls me that."

"I like it. *Lapushka*." She drew out the second syllable. "It's sweet."

"Better than *mon petit chou*. French for my little cabbage," he added when she frowned.

"I thought you didn't know French."

"That was the extent of my knowledge."

"At least now I have something to call Piper next time she calls."

Stuart didn't answer. A faraway look found its way to his face. Patience touched his cheek to call him back to the present. "You're thinking about what Ana told us this afternoon, aren't you?"

"Grandpa Theodore took so much from her.

She could have had a completely different life." He cast his eyes to the cushion, but not before she caught a flash of regret. "I keep wondering if there isn't some way I could fix the damage he caused."

"How? Unless you can turn back time, I don't think you can."

"Actually…" With a moan that could best be described as reluctant, Stuart rolled onto his side. The separation wasn't more than a few inches, but Patience felt the distance immediately and shivered. "I was thinking about that this afternoon."

"About turning back time?"

"Sort of."

Now he had her interest. She shifted onto her side as well, propping herself on one elbow so as to give him her full attention. "What do you mean?"

"I was thinking about the painting we saw in the photograph. Ana said Nigel painted all sorts of studies of her."

"Yes, but she also said your grandfather paid someone to buy all of them."

"But what if he didn't? I mean, what if he wasn't able to buy them all. Ana made it sound like there were a lot of paintings and sketches. It's possible one or two of them survived. Grandpa Theodore was powerful, but he wasn't omnipotent. In spite of what he thought."

"Do you really think a painting exists?"

"It's possible, and if one does, then Ana could have back a piece of what she lost. Might not be much, but…"

It was a wonderful, beautiful gesture that deepened the feelings that were rapidly taking control of Patience's heart. "But Nigel died years ago,' she reminded him. "How would we ever find out about his paintings?"

"We can at least try. I did a little searching on the internet this afternoon. Apparently Nigel had a sister."

"Really? Is she still alive?"

"Alive and living in Paris. If anyone knows what happened to his artwork, it would be her.

All we need is for someone to go talk to her. You wouldn't happen to have any ideas who we could call, do you?" he asked, brushing the bangs from her face.

"Funny you should ask—I do." She matched his grin. "I'm sure Piper would be glad to help. She knows how important Ana is to me. I'll call her tomorrow. With luck, she can arrange to talk to Nigel's sister this week."

"That would be great. Thank you."

He didn't have to thank her. "After everything Ana has done for me, this is nothing. I'd love to find this painting as much as you." And give back to the woman who saved her a piece of her soul mate that was bigger than a box of memories and a string of cats bearing his name.

Thinking of the cats made her giggle. "What's so funny?" Stuart asked.

"Nothing. I was thinking, if the cats all had Nigel's personality, does that mean he never stopped eating?"

"Interesting question. We'll have to ask Ana someday.

"In the meantime," he said, rising above her. "It's still the middle of the night in Paris. We've got a few hours to kill before we can think about calling your sister."

"Is that so?"

"Uh-huh." He gripped her waist and quickly flipped her beneath him, causing Patience to let out a high-pitched squeal. "Looks like we'll have to find something to pass the time," he said, dipping his head.

Patience met him halfway.

Despite claiming her older sister "owed her," Piper was more than happy to visit Nigel's sister, just as Patience knew she would be. "Stuart and I really appreciate this," she said to the younger woman.

"Stuart, huh?" Piper's face loomed large as she leaned toward the screen. "How are things going with the two of you? Is he still cool with, you know, the club?"

Patience's mind flashed to a few hours before, in Stuart's bed. "Seems to be," she replied.

"See? I told you he'd understand. It's not like you went to work in that place because you liked dancing naked on tables."

"Of course, I didn't," Patience replied with a wince. She wondered if the memory would ever stop making her stomach churn. "And you're right. Stuart says he understands."

"Wait—what do you mean 'says he understands'? Don't you believe him?"

"No, I believe him. Stuart's been great."

"Then what's wrong?"

"Nothing." Patience shook her head. How could she explain that Stuart being great was the problem. He was too great while she was...well, she sure as heck didn't feel worthy. Sooner or later, this dream had to end. A soft sigh escaped her lips. Too late, she remembered Piper was on the other end of the line.

"Patience?"

Blinking, she came face-to-face with Piper's scowl.

"What aren't you telling me?" her sister asked.

"Um…" She bit her lip and prayed her sister's old cell phone camera wouldn't pick up her blush.

It was a fruitless wish. "Oh, my God! Is something going on between you and your boss?"

"He's not my boss," Patience said quickly. "He's my boss's great-nephew."

They were splitting hairs and they both knew it, which was why Piper asked, "What exactly is the difference?"

"The difference…" There was no difference, but she didn't want to admit it. Calling Stuart her boss only reminded her they weren't from the same world, a reality she was trying to ignore for as long as possible. Acknowledging that reality would only lead to others, like Patience not being good enough for him. "The difference would be the same as you dating either your boss or his next-door neighbor." she finally said.

Just as she knew she would, Piper rolled her eyes at the lame example. "Please. The only neighbor I've met is an eleven-year-old boy, and my boss doesn't even…"

"Doesn't even what?" For some reason, her sister had stopped midsentence, and her gaze was focused on a point off camera. "Piper?"

"Sorry, I lost track of what I was about to say. And you still haven't answered my question. Are you dating Stuart Duchenko?"

"For now, yes."

"No way! That's great!" Piper beamed from ear to ear. "I'm so happy for you."

"Don't go making a big deal. We're having fun together, that's all. It's nothing serious."

Of course she still hadn't mentioned the other thing. After Stuart distracted her yesterday—not that she'd fought too hard—there hadn't been another good moment. Then again, when was there a good time to share something so humiliating? It wasn't exactly something you could blurt out. *Hey, Stuart, by the way, dancing naked wasn't the only thing in my past I didn't tell you about. There's also this little police matter...*

She switched the subject back to Nigel Rougeau's sister and hoped Piper believed her.

At least one of them should.

* * *

"And this," Stuart said, "is the firm library. Home away from home for any decent first-year associate."

He snuck a kiss to Patience's temple while pointing out the shelves, causing her knees to wobble slightly. Not because of the kiss but from the intimacy it implied.

"Was it yours?" She pictured his dark head bent over the books late at night.

"Are you kidding? See that desk by the window? If you sit in the chair, you can still feel the imprint from my butt cheeks."

Patience choked back a snort, causing a pair of heads to look in their direction, only to return to their work as soon as they spied Stuart. "Don't look now, but I think they're afraid of you."

"Well, I can be pretty scary, you know."

"I know I was terrified when I first met you."

"I could tell by the way you sauced off."

"That's not even a real word." Giggling, she slapped his sleeve. One of the heads looked up again, and she couldn't help indulging in a moment of smug pride. *That's right*, she wanted to say, *your boss is entertaining me.*

It was an illusion, of course, this image of being a couple, but she was willing to let herself enjoy the fantasy for as long as it lasted. Later today, Ana would be coming home, and soon after Stuart would be moving out, bringing an end to their affair. When that happened, she would confront the emotions she was fighting to keep buried.

Until then, she'd let the illusion have control.

"The partner's dining room is next door," Stuart said. "Would you rather eat in there or in my office?"

That's why she was here. With Ana returning home, Stuart had invited her to lunch to discuss what she needed to do to get the brownstone ready. "You're the host. I'll let you decide."

"My office it is. That way I can ravish you after we eat," he whispered in her ear.

Patience's knees wobbled again. The way his voice grew husky, she could listen to his whisper all day long. "Sounds good to me."

"What part? The eating or the ravishing?" Either. Both. She welcomed the privacy, too. Previous moment aside, she felt uncomfortable walking around Stuart's law firm. Although she'd exchanged her jeans for an ankle-length skirt and tank top, she still felt out of place amid the power suits. "What are you talking about?" Stuart had remarked when she'd mentioned her fears. "No one expects my date to look like she's heading to court."

"They would if she was a lawyer," she countered.

"But she's not. She's you."

He had no idea how his response made her heart soar.

"Bob was looking for you," a woman called to them when they reached his office.

"I know," Stuart replied. "I got his emails. If it's about the Peavey case, tell him to send the brief directly to John Greenwood."

"He said this was about another project. A report you asked him to assemble."

There was a sudden stutter in his step. While they weren't touching, Patience could still feel

Stuart's body tense. "Oh," he replied. "Tell him I'll talk with him later." Even his voice sounded tight.

"I'm keeping you from something important, aren't I?" she asked.

"Nothing that can't wait."

But she was. His whole demeanor had changed on a dime. Lighthearted Stuart had disappeared behind a shadow. All of a sudden, he was frowning, the playful gleam gone from his eyes.

"Seriously, if you have work to do, I can—"

"No." He practically shouted the word. For some reason, it made the hair on her neck stand on end. "Whatever Bob has to say can wait."

"But if he's trying so hard to talk with you…" Multiple emails and personal visits—it had to be important.

Stuart shook his head. "I already know what he wants to tell me, and it's not important at all."

"Okay. If you say so." No need pressing the issue, even though she wasn't sure she believed him. "Bob can wait."

"Exactly."

Stuart's office was a mirror image of him. Attractive and elegant. If this was the reward, no wonder those associates worked so hard.

She stood in the center of the room while he closed his office door and then turned to her with a mischievous grin.

"Are we planning to eat?" she asked him.

"Eventually." Taking her hand, he led her to the luxurious leather chair that dominated the back of his desk. "First things first. I believe I said something about ravishing."

"I distinctly remember you saying after we eat."

"Sue me. I lied."

She would have made a joke about being in the perfect place to do so had he not completely derailed her thoughts by slipping his arms around her waist. She tumbled onto his lap without argument.

His eagerness never ceased to amaze her. Every time he kissed her felt like the first time, passionate and needy.

She let out a whimper when he broke away.

"Sadly, not being able to lock my door prevents a proper ravishing. That will have to wait until later."

"Your aunt will be home."

"She has to sleep eventually. And, if I recall, they're installing her bed on the first floor, which means we can be as loud as we want." He slipped off the strap of her tank top and nipped at the exposed skin.

Goodness, but she would going to miss this when he left. Putting her hands on his shoulders, Patience pushed gently away. One of them had to add some space; otherwise, it wouldn't matter whether his door locked or not.

"I thought we needed to talk about Ana's new living arrangements," she said. Stuart groaned, but he didn't argue.

"The medical supply company delivered the bed this morning," she continued. "Is Ana okay with the arrangement?" After discussing it, she and Stuart had decided to move his aunt to the first floor for the next few weeks. Dr. O'Hara had been concerned about her going up and down stairs. Stuart and Patience were concerned she might trip over Nigel again.

"She's not crazy about the idea, but I think Dr. O'Hara convinced her she was doing the smart thing. I told her you'd bring down a lot of her personal items and set up the front sitting room as much like her bedroom as possible."

"Linens and nightstand are already down. And when I left, Nigel had taken up residence on the bed." She'd passed the cat curled up in the center of the mattress, the same location he claimed on Ana's regular bed.

"So long as she has Nigel, she'll be more than comfortable," Stuart replied. "Speaking of...have you spoken to your sister yet?"

"No. I got a message from her this morning saying she wanted to video chat, but we were unable to connect. I don't know if she's managed to look into Ana's painting, though."

"She has. I got an email from her just before you arrived."

"You did? Why didn't you tell me?"

The index finger trailing down her arm gave her the answer. He'd been distracted.

"Did she say if she learned anything?" she asked, ignoring the goose bumps ghosting across her skin.

A slow smile broke across Stuart's face. "Looks like we were right. A dealer did buy the contents of Nigel's studio right after his death—I'm guessing that's the man Grandpa Theodore hired— but it turns out that Nigel sold at least a couple pieces before his death. She gave Piper the name of the gallery owner who brokered the transaction. Piper and her boss were going to talk to him tomorrow."

"That's great! Wait." Patience paused. "Did you say her boss was helping her?" To hear Piper talk, the two of them barely had contact.

"Maybe he's helping her translate."

That would make sense. Piper's French was shaky. "Let's keep our fingers crossed the gallery owner kept decent records."

"Fingers, toes, and anything else you can think

of," Stuart replied. "I really want to make this happen for Ana."

"Same here." Especially if success meant Stuart would have a smile, as well. Patience was pretty sure she'd do anything to see that.

Stuart didn't take two-hour lunches. Not unless there was a business meeting involved. But, with Patience, the time simply got away from him. Moreover, he didn't care. If he didn't have work to finish before Ana's discharge, he would have been perfectly happy to let the lunch go on for three or four hours. The woman was so damn easy to talk to.

Easy to do a lot of things with, he thought with a smile.

You, pal, are in deep, aren't you? For once, he let his subconscious speak freely. He *was* in deep, and, to his amazement, the thought didn't set off alarm bells. Why should it? Patience wasn't Gloria. Patience didn't pretend to be something she wasn't or tell him what she thought he wanted to hear. Instead, she was content to be with him—

the real him. The one who wore thick glasses and talked about sunset differentials. Even at his most besotted, to steal his aunt's word, Gloria didn't make his insides feel light and joyful, the way Patience did. So, Stuart didn't freak out at the notion he might be falling. In fact, he could see himself falling a lot deeper.

Someone cleared his throat. Stuart looked to the door, saw who it was and cringed. "Hey, Bob. Come on in."

The overly tall, overly eager looking attorney stepped inside and closed the door behind him. No doubt meant as a gesture of confidentiality, it made Stuart wince nonetheless. "The investigator tracked down the information you needed," he said, brandishing a thin manila envelope. "I know it took a little longer than expected, but we had a couple big cases come through, and since this was personal and you hadn't followed up…"

"I thought I sent you an email telling you to cancel the investigation."

"You—you did?" The color drained from Bob's

face. Associates hoping to be on the fast track hated to make mistakes, Bob more than most. "I didn't see one."

"A few weeks ago." The Saturday following the dinner dance. Stuart distinctly remembered typing out the message before going to bed. Right before Nigel jumped up and demanded attention.

Damn. Was it possible he hadn't hit Send? Now two people who didn't need to know were aware of Patience's secret.

Bob mistook his wiping his hand across his face for displeasure. "I am so sorry. The note must have gotten buried somehow...I..." He thrust the envelope at Stuart. "Are you sure you don't need this information? I mean, it's pretty interesting reading, I'll say that."

"You read it?"

Again Bob paled. "Um, only to make sure the report was complete. I wasn't trying to pry..."

Like hell he wasn't. The investigator's notes were probably too salacious to pass up. He gave Bob a dismissive look, letting the associate know he was unhappy with his performance. "Doesn't matter," he made a point of saying. "I already know everything the investigator might have found."

"You do?" Bob said. "Even the criminal record?"

Criminal record? Please no. Stuart squeezed the arms of his chair tight enough to snap them. It took every ounce of his control and then some to keep his face free of reaction. "Yes, even that."

"Oh. Okay. I'll go finish the brief for Greenwood then."

"You do that," Stuart replied. "And Bob?" Man, but it was hard to talk with nausea rising in his throat. "If you ever get a personal project from a partner again? Mind your own business."

The associate nodded before exiting as quickly as possible. Leaving Stuart alone.

With the manila envelope.

It had to be a mistake. Patience had told him everything, right? And he trusted her.

But what if…the possibility made him gag.

Only one way to be certain. He tore open the envelope.

"Dammit!" He slammed his fist on the desk, ignoring the pain shooting to his elbow. It was nothing compared to the hurt tearing through his insides. There, fastened to the top of the report, was everything he didn't want to know.

"All right, Nigel, let's get this straight. This is Ana's new bed, not yours. Meaning you will give her space to lie down when she and Stuart get home from the hospital, okay?"

Which, Patience checked the clock on the mantel, should be in an hour or so. She smoothed the wrinkles from Ana's comforter. The setup might not be ideal, but it would work for a month. Who knows? Ana might decide she liked living on the first floor.

We can be as loud as we want. A delicious shiver ran down her spine as she remembered Stuart's comment after Dr. O'Hara suggested the new arrangement. "Might as well make the most of what we have while we have it, right, Nigel?" she said, combing her fingers through Nigel's fur.

Suddenly, the front door slammed with a force

so hard it made the frame rattle against the wall. Stuart appeared in the doorway, wild-eyed and out of breath.

"Stuart, what's wrong?" Instinctively, she took a step backward. He looked like a madman. The pupils in his eyes were blown wide, and while she'd seen them black with desire, she'd never seen them like this. "Did something happen to Ana?"

"Ana's fine."

"Then what?" This was not the man she had spent lunch sharing kisses with. This man looked like he wanted to…

Oh, no. She spied the crumpled papers in his fist. Pain began spreading across her chest, sharp like a heart attack. Why couldn't the past have stayed buried for a little while longer?

"I can explain," she said.

"Oh, I bet you can." His voice had gone dead. "I bet you have a whole slew of explanations at the ready."

"Stuart—"

"I trusted you," he spit. "When you said you

told me everything, I believed you, but you were lying."

"No," she said, shaking her head. "I was telling the truth."

"Oh, yeah?" He stalked closer, waving the papers in his fist like they were a club. "Then tell me. Why do I have a police record telling me you were a prostitute?"

CHAPTER TEN

THE ACCUSATION HUNG between them, a fat, ugly cloud. Patience wished she could turn herself into Nigel. He'd run under the bed when Stuart slammed the door.

"This is what you were really hiding, wasn't it? You didn't want Ana to know who she'd hired. What she'd hired."

What she'd hired? How dared he? "I am not a prostitute."

"Your police record says otherwise."

"Police records don't tell the whole story." A few sentences typed on a form. How could it possibly cover all the details?

Tell that to Stuart, though. His outburst seemed to let out some of his steam, making the anger more of a slow boil. Patience preferred the outrage. Folding his arms, he settled in a nearby chair, his eyes burning holes in her skin.

"Then by all means, enlighten me," he said. "I can't wait to hear the long version."

"Why should I bother? You've obviously made up your mind." Worse, she wasn't entirely sure she could blame him after hiding the truth the way she had.

"Try me."

Patience almost laughed, the comment was so close to his words the night of the dance. The night she should have come clean. He'd been willing to listen then. Now she wasn't so sure.

In his chair, Stuart sat waiting. Her own personal judge and jury.

She took a deep breath. "You ever been to a place like Feathers? It's not some upscale bachelors' club. It's a dive, with divey people. Some of the girls—a lot of the girls—did stuff on the side to make extra cash."

"But not you."

"No!" she snarled. She got it. He was angry and hurt, but to even suggest... How many nights had she spent in his arms offering herself to him, body and soul? She didn't share herself like that with just anyone, and he should know that.

Stuart must have realized he'd crossed the line, as his voice lost its sharp edge. "How did you get lumped in with the others then?"

"One night, the cops raided the club, and hauled us all downtown. My lawyer said it would be too hard to fight the charge and I'd be better off pleading out to avoid jail time."

"Too hard for whom? You or him?"

It was the first civil thing he'd said since walking in, and it was a question she'd asked herself dozens of time. "I just wanted the whole thing to go away so I did what he said. I didn't want to risk breaking my promise to Piper.

"And that," she said, sinking onto the edge of the bed, "is the long version."

Neither of them said anything for several minutes. Patience stared at the floral duvet, counting the various blossoms. A tail brushed her ankle. Nigel making his escape to the kitchen. The lucky guy

Finally, Stuart broke the silence. "If all this is true, why did you lie? I might have understood if you'd told me first."

"Because I wanted to forget the night ever happened. I felt dirty enough. To admit I not only danced like a cheap whore, but I was arrested like one, too?" No matter how tightly she wrapped her arms around her midsection, her stomach still ached every time she thought about it. "Do you have any idea how it felt the other night, having to tell you about my pathetic past? I wanted to salvage a little bit of dignity." And also cling to him a little bit longer.

None of that mattered now. Patience had seen the loathing on Stuart's face when he walked in.

"All I ever wanted from this job was respect."

"You had my respect."

Had. Past tense. Her insides ripped in two. Hadn't she known from the beginning getting involved with Stuart was a bad idea. *Don't drop your defenses*, she'd told herself. *The crash would be worse if you let yourself care.*

Well, she hadn't listened, and the crash was killing her.

Stuart stood and crossed to the window. "I trusted you." The same words he'd said when he first came in. Violating his trust had been her biggest crime of all.

Except…

"Did you?" she asked suddenly. "Did you really trust me?"

"You know I did. I told you about Gloria, for crying out loud."

"Then how did you find out about my record?" Last time she looked, there wasn't a criminal record fairy handing out information. A person had to go searching for it. "I don't believe it. You had me investigated didn't you?"

"I—" He couldn't even look her in the eye.

"You did. Unbelievable." Sitting here, making her feel bad about her violating *his* trust, when all the time… "Face it, *lapushka*." She drew the word out as sourly as she could. "You never trusted me all, did you?"

"That's not true." Stuart shook his head.

Right. And she was the Queen of England. Suddenly, the brownstone was much too small for the two of them. She needed to leave right now.

"Where are you going?" Stuart asked when she stalked toward the foyer.

"Out." Unless she was fired, she still had the right to come and go as she pleased. "I need some air."

She noticed Stuart didn't try to stop her. Looked like the fantasy truly was over.

Well, like she always said, Prince Charming ain't walking through that door. Instead, *she* was walking out.

"Patience?" Soft though it was, Ana's voice still managed to echo through the brownstone. "Where is she? I thought you said she was waiting for us at home?"

"I thought she was," Stuart told her. A lie. He'd been *hoping* Patience was waiting for them. He had no idea if she'd ever come back after walking out.

This was his fault. If he hadn't been such a jerk

when he'd found out about her arrest. But he'd been hurt, and he'd lashed out.

A soft meow sounded behind them. "Nigel, my sweetie pie. Did you miss Mommy?" His aunt hobbled over to the stairway. "He looks like he's lost weight. Don't you think?"

"Maybe. I don't know." At the moment, he was more concerned with Patience's whereabouts. "Maybe she went to the store."

Ana was trying to scratch an excited Nigel's head without falling over. "But she knew we were on our way. Why wouldn't she wait until we got here?"

"Perhaps she went to get something for your return. Tea, maybe." But he'd already discounted his theory soon as the words left his mouth. "Or maybe she's upstairs and can't hear us in her room." An equally lame suggestion, but he clung to the possibility.

"Tell you what," he said, scooping up Nigel. "Why don't I show you what we've set up in the front parlor? Then, while you and Nigel are having a good reunion, I'll go see if I can track down Patience."

But he was pretty sure he knew the answer. The air in the brownstone was different; the silence thicker than usual. By the time he went upstairs and spied Patience's open bedroom door, he was certain.

He stood in the doorway while his heart shattered. The bed where they'd made love this morning had been stripped to the mattress, the bedding folded in neat piles waiting to be washed. She'd left the closet door open. One lone hanger, the only sign the space had ever held clothes, lay on the floor.

A blue scarf hung on the doorknob. He recognized it as the one Patience wore to the dinner dance. Balling the cloth in his fist, he pressed it to his cheek, and inhaled deep. He remembered the way her scent had teased him while they'd danced. The memory mocked him now. The pain in his chest threatened to cut him at the knees.

Dear God, but the house already felt emptier. *And it was all his fault.*

On the bureau lay an envelope with Ana's name scrawled across the front. No goodbye for him, he thought sadly. He didn't deserve one.

"Is she upstairs?" Ana asked when he returned.

"No. She's gone."

"What do you mean gone? I don't understand." Her eyes narrowed when he handed her the envelope. He was doing a lousy job of hiding his feelings, and she knew it. "What's going on Stuart?"

"It's complicated," he replied. "You should read the letter."

"Do you know what's in it?"

"No." But he could guess.

"What does she mean she couldn't bear to face me after I found out?" Ana looked up with a frown. "Found out about what?"

It was the question he'd been dreading. "Patience..." Staring at his hands, he searched for the right words. "Turns out she was keeping secrets." Briefly, he told her about Patience's arrest and her job at Feathers, doing the best he could to leave out the gory details. When he finished, Ana looked back to the letter that was on her lap. "I'm sorry, Tetya."

"I figured her story had to be something pretty awful for her to lie about it."

"She was afraid—" He whipped his head around. "You knew she was lying?"

"Of course, I did. Surely you don't think I'm that naive." Her glare chased off any possible response. "I could tell she was hiding something during her interview. It was obvious she didn't know a thing about being a proper housekeeper. And the way she stuttered on about forgetting her agency paperwork…the girl is not a very good liar, you know. After she left, I spoke to the agency, and they told me the real candidate had gotten stuck on the subway."

Stuart owed his aunt an apology. She was far sharper than he gave her credit.

"Wait," he said, backing off that thought. "If you knew she was lying, why did you hire her? Why didn't you call her out on the story?"

"Because the poor dear was clearly desperate. Leaping at the chance to clean house?"

"Still, for all you knew, she could have been trying to rob you." The questions were moot at this point. He was simply looking for grounds to justify his mistrust. Hoping for some sliver of a reason to prove he wasn't an arrogant, jaded fool.

"Nonsense," Ana replied. "Patience couldn't hurt a fly. Anyone who spends five minutes with her can tell that."

Yes, they could. Even he, with all his suspicion, had recognized her gentle sweetness. It's why he'd fallen so hard in spite of himself.

"Besides, Nigel liked her and he doesn't like just anyone. That alone told me I could trust her. As for not asking her story…I figured when the time came, she would tell me what I needed to know."

In other words, his aunt had decided based on the opinion of a cat who, sadly enough, was a better judge of character than he was.

"In a lot of ways, Patience reminds me of the animals at the shelter," she told him. "Lost and looking for a place to call home. I know it was a rash decision—a dangerous one, even—but I couldn't turn her away."

"When you put it that way…" It didn't sound so rash at all. Simply confident in the goodness of human nature. Something he'd always had trouble with. He thought he'd conquered his mistrust, but apparently not.

"She has a way of getting under your skin, doesn't she?" Now the guilt arrived, strong and harsh. He'd managed to do what his aunt couldn't: chase Patience away. He'd let her sweetness frighten him and turn him into a bully.

"I've really screwed things up, haven't I?" he said.

"Yes, you have."

Ana never did believe in mincing words. "What do I do?" He looked to her face, hoping in her wisdom she'd have a solution.

"For starters, you can get me my housekeeper back. I care too much for her to lose her."

"Me, too," Stuart whispered. He should never

have overreacted the way he did when he'd read Bob's report. If he'd acted calmly, Patience might be here with him right now. Instead, he'd let his heart give in to suspicion. And she was gone.

"She's never going to forgive me."

"You'll never know until you try."

When he shook his head, she reached over and took his hands, her gnarled grip stronger than he expected. "Listen to me. I had the chance to fight for my Nigel. I didn't and I lost him forever. I don't want to see the same thing happen to you. You have already missed out on so many years of happiness because of Theodore and that gold digger he married. Patience is your second chance. Don't be like me, lapushka—fight for her."

His aunt was right. He couldn't give up on Patience. He had to find her if only to apologize for being an ass. "How did he track her down, though? He doubted she'd left a forwarding address at the bottom of her goodbye note. But....

There was one person Patience would contact no matter where she ran off to. One person she would never desert. And he had that person's email address. A kernel of hope took root inside him.

Rising, he kissed Ana on the cheek. "I'll be right back."

"Where are you going?"

"I've got to send an important note to someone in France."

"You look lousy."

"Back at you." Patience knew exactly how she looked. Tired and depressed. Same way she felt. "The beds at this place are like boards on stilts. I was tossing and turning half the night." She missed the big comfy bed she had at Ana's.

She missed a lot of things she had back at Ana's.

But that was in the past. With a swipe of her hand, she brushed away her bangs and the painful thoughts. "I've got possible good news, though. The front desk clerk told me they're hiring at the new Super Shopper's Mart. I'm going to go apply today."

"Good luck."

"Thanks." She'd need it. She couldn't afford to hide away in a hotel room forever. Eventually, she was going to have to find a new job and a new place to live. Preferably soon, before she drained her savings and found herself living in her car. Again.

Funny how things came full circle.

"I just hope they don't ask for a lot of references. Or ask too much about my previous position."

"Maybe if you called Ana…"

"No." Patience cut that suggestion right off. That possibility died when she'd walked out.

She hadn't meant to leave so abruptly. Not at first, anyway. When she'd stormed out of the brownstone, she'd truly intended to just clear her head. Problem was, the more she walked around Beacon Hill, the more upset she got. At Stuart for being so damn suspicious of everybody. At the world for being so unfair in the first place.

But mostly at herself for being stupid enough to

think she could bury the past. And for letting her guard down. She'd let herself care—more than care—and now her insides were being shredded for her foolishness. In the end, she'd decided she couldn't face seeing Stuart or Ana again, and so when Stuart had left for the hospital, she'd packed her things.

"Don't you think you're being drastic?" Piper asked.

"Trust me, I'm not. You should have seen Stuart's face," she added in a soft voice. For as long as she lived, she wouldn't forget how the betrayal and anger darkened his features.

"Probably because he was mad you didn't tell him. Stinks when people keep information from you."

Patience winced. "I know. I'm sorry." The other night she'd broken down and told Piper about the arrest. Her sister had been ticked off over being kept in the dark, too, although she'd softened when Patience had explained how it wasn't news you shared with your preteen sister.

The thing was, Piper was right. If she'd told Ana everything from the beginning, she wouldn't be in this position. Granted, she probably wouldn't have gotten the job, but she also wouldn't have had to deal with Ana's disappointment. Or with Stuart's. Which, when she thought about the past couple weeks, would have been the best thing of all.

Sure would hurt less, that's for sure.

"I'm not really upset anymore," Piper told her. "Stuart might not be, either. Maybe he decided that the past doesn't matter."

"Right, that's why he had me investigated. Because my past doesn't matter." She still couldn't believe he'd crossed that line. Well, actually, she could believe it. Stuart had said from the beginning he had trust issues. Still… "Who does he think he is, judging me? I may not have made fantastic decisions, but I always had the best intentions. I got you an education, and I kept us off the streets."

"Hey, no arguments from me," her sister replied. "I think you're awesome."

And to think she had been feeling guilty about not telling him. Turns out her subconscious knew best. The only thing telling him about the arrest would have accomplished would be to put the regret in his eyes that much faster. At least this way, she'd eked out a few more days with him.

"I never should have let myself…"

"Let yourself what?" Naturally Piper heard her. When would she learn to keep her thoughts quiet?

She considered brushing the comment off, but Piper wouldn't let her. When she was a kid, she'd made Patience repeat every under-the-breath phrase ever muttered. Maybe talking would lessen the ache in the chest. "Let myself start to care," she said.

"You really like him, don't you?"

Way more than liked. She missed him the way she would miss breathing. "Not that it matters. I told you before, we were having a fling, nothing more, I mean, face it—even if I'd told him everything from the start, he could never seriously love someone like me. We come from completely different places."

"So? Why can't people from different worlds fall in love?"

"Do they? When's the last time someone from our neighborhood got swept off their feet by a millionaire?" *Prince Charming ain't walking through that door.*

"That's not what you used to tell me."

"You're different," Patience immediately replied. "I raised you to be better than the neighborhood."

"I know. You always said I was just as good as the next person."

"You are."

"Then, aren't you?"

Closing her eyes, Patience let out a long, slow breath. "This is different."

"How?"

Because, she wanted to say, the world wasn't black-and-white. Equality in a human sense didn't mean equal in the eyes of society. And while Stuart had no right to judge her as a person, there was a huge difference between not judging someone and falling in love with them.

"Trust me, it just is. A guy like Stuart doesn't want to spend the rest of his life with an ex-stripper."

Before either sister could keep the argument going, a knock sounded on her hotel door. "Who on earth would be banging on my door this time of morning?" Patience asked, frowning. Housekeeping didn't start for another hour.

"Patience, are you in there?"

The sound of Stuart's voice came through the wood, causing her heart to panic. "It's Stuart," she whispered. "He's here." How had he managed to track her down? The only person who knew her location was...

"You didn't," she said with a glare.

"He asked me to contact him as soon as I knew where you were staying. He wants to talk with you."

"Patience, I know you're in there. Please open the door."

She looked over her shoulder before glaring at her laptop where her sister's face was the picture of apology. "What makes you think I want to talk with him?"

"How about the fact that you look like hell? Give him five minutes. What if he's sorry?"

"Sorry, not sorry—I told you, it doesn't make a difference."

"And I think you should hear him out."

"I'm going to keep knocking until you answer," Stuart called from outside.

He would, too. A knot lodged itself at the base of her skull. A ball of tension just waiting to become a headache. Patience squeezed the back of her neck, trying to push the tension away, but the feeling was as stubborn as the man banging on her hotel door.

"Patience?"

"Fine. One minute! I am so going to kill you when you get back to Boston," she hissed at her sister.

"I love you, too," Piper replied.

Whatever. Patience slapped the laptop closed. Might as well get this over with. A quick glance at the mirror told her she really did look terrible.

She started to comb her fingers through her hair, thought better of it and went to the door.

"What?" she asked, through the chained opening.

Stuart's blue eyes peered down at her. "May I come in?"

"Anything you need to say, I'm sure you can say from out there." Where she was safer. The mere sound of his voice had her insides quaking. Goodness knows what standing close to him would do.

"You sure you want me airing our dirty laundry so everyone else in the place can hear us?" he asked.

Damn. He had a point. "Fine. Five minutes." Sighing, she unlatched the door and let him in. Immediately, she knew it was a mistake. He had on his weekend clothes. Faded jeans and a T-shirt. The look made him appear far more approachable than his suit. She didn't want him approachable. She wanted to keep her distance.

He jammed his hands into his back pockets. "How are you?" he asked.

"I was doing fine until you got my sister involved," she replied.

"You don't look like you're doing fine."

"How I look isn't your business anymore." Nevertheless, she pulled her sweater tightly around her, feeling exposed in her T-shirt and sleep shorts. "What's so important that you needed to track me down?"

"You left without saying goodbye."

"I left a note."

"For Ana."

"Maybe Ana's the only person I wanted to say goodbye to."

"Ouch."

If he expected an apology, he was mistaken. "Is that all you came about? To critique how I said goodbye?"

"No. I came to find out why you left."

He was kidding, right? "Isn't it obvious?" She started to make the bed, fussing with the sheets the alternative to losing her temper. Did you really think I would stick around so Ana could fire me for lying to her?"

"No one was going to fire you."

Patience stopped her fussing. "Okay, pity me then."

Stepping away from the door, Stuart walked to the opposite side of the bed. The queen-size space suddenly felt too small a buffer zone. The rumpled sheets did nothing but remind her what it felt like to be under the covers with his arms wrapped around her.

"No one was going to pity you, either," he said. "Ana knew from the very beginning. Well, not the specifics, but she knew you lied your way into the job."

"How?" She wasn't sure she should believe him.

"Apparently you're not that good an actress."

What did he say the other day? Body language always gives people away. Here she thought she was fooling everyone, when in reality the only fool was her.

She sank to the bed, her back to him. "If Ana knew...why did she hire me?"

"You know Ana and her thing for strays."

Yeah, she did. Ana believed all creatures deserved a good home. Obviously, she'd believed Patience did, too. A lump rose in her throat, bringing tears. Ana was a greater gift in her life than Patience ever realized.

Suddenly, she felt like the world's biggest jerk. "You're right. I owed her a better goodbye. I'll call her."

"Better yet, why not come back?"

"You know I can't do that."

"Why not? I told you, she doesn't care. *I* don't care."

Behind her, she heard his soft cough. "Look, Ana's not the reason I came. I came to apologize for the way I overreacted the other day. I was a jerk. I should have trusted that you had a good reason for not telling me about the arrest."

"You hired an investigator."

"Yes, I did," he said. "When I first got to town and was worried about Ana. But that was before I got to know you."

"Stop." Next, he'd start saying how much he'd come to like and admire her or some other meaningless sweet talk. Her heart was hurting enough as it was. "I get it. Really, I do. Shame on me for not expecting it."

"Excuse me?"

He came around the foot of the bed until he stood by her knees. Patience immediately fought the urge to scoot backward, to where their personal spaces couldn't merge.

With a swipe of her hair, she gave her best imitation of disinterest. "In a way, the timing couldn't have been better. I mean, we both know we were ending things soon. This way we got the messy part over with."

"What are you talking about?"

"Do you really need me to spell it out for you?" She had to give him credit—he actually sounded incredulous. "A millionaire and an ex-stripper who cleans toilets? Hardly a fairy tale. I knew from the beginning it was temporary."

He met her attitude with one of his own. Arms folded, he scowled down at her with eyes that pinned her to the spot. "Wow, you've got everything all worked out, don't you?"

"I'm a realist. I know how the world works."

"And how would you know what I was thinking? You didn't stick around long enough to find out. Hell, you would have walked out the night of the dinner dance if I hadn't pressed you for an explanation."

He leaned into her face, bringing his eyes and lips dangerously close. "You know," he said, his voice low, "you keep talking about me not trusting you, but I'm not the only one with trust issues. You were so certain you knew what I was thinking, you didn't give me the chance to give you the benefit of the doubt. Maybe, if you'd told me about your arrest. Let me in…"

"I let you in as much as I dared," she told him. "If I told you every lousy thing that's happened in my life, you'd…"

"What? Be disgusted. Throw you out?"

"Yes."

"Bull. You only let me in when circumstances pressured you. If Chablis hadn't crossed our paths, I'd never have found out about Feathers.

Trust works both ways, babe." Taking a deep breath, he stepped away.

Patience hugged her midsection. Without Stuart's presence to warm it, the air became cold and empty feeling. "Big words coming from a guy who was still investigating me after we started sleeping together," she murmured.

Her words hit their mark, and he winced. A small consolation. "That was a mistake," he said. "I meant to call Bob off."

"Of course, you did." He simply forgot, right? "Let me guess, the voice in your head telling you I wasn't good enough wouldn't let you. A woman with her background—no way she could be any good," she whispered, mimicking.

"That's bull."

"Is it?" She wondered. "Why else would a person 'forget' to stop an investigation?"

"Because I was distracted."

"By what? What could possibly be that distracting?" Why she was even bothering to push the issue she didn't know, other than that she needed to hear him admit the truth.

But his answer wasn't what she expected. "You," he said. "You distracted me."

"With what? My banging body."

"No, by being yourself. I forgot to call Bob because I was too busy falling in love with you."

Love? This had to be his idea of a cruel joke. He couldn't really be in love with her. Could he?

Slowly, she raised her eyes and looked into his. There was so much honesty in their blueness it hurt. "How can you love me? I'm—

"Sweet, wonderful, smart..."

"But the things I did. The life I led."

"Sweetheart, those are things you did. They aren't you, not the way you think," he told her. Suddenly, he was in her space again, his hands cradling her cheeks. "I'm in love with Patience Rush. The woman who was willing to do anything, including sacrifice herself, to keep her sister safe. Who survived despite all the hell life threw at her. The woman who was strong enough to pull her and her sister up from that world. That's the Patience I'm in love with."

A tear slipped down Patience's cheek. "When I think about all those years in the club…"

"Shh. Don't think about them. They're in the past." He kissed her. As gentle and sweet a kiss as she ever experienced. She wished she could hold on to the moment forever.

"Come home, Patience," he whispered.

Fighting not to cry, she broke away. "I can't…"

Stuart looked like she'd slapped him. Disappointed and hurt. His expression made the ache in her heart worse. "Can't or won't?" he challenged.

"Can't." Might as well be honest. The past was too much a part of her to let it go. What if a week from now he changed his mind when he'd had time to think? The rejection would be too much to bear.

"I think you should go," she told him.

"Patience…"

She shook him off before her resolve could crumble. "Please. If you respect me at all…"

They were the magic words. Stuart took back his touch. "Fine."

He stopped when he got to the door. Patience didn't turn around, but she heard the pause in his step. "Just remember, all my anger and mistrust was because you were keeping secrets. I never once judged you for your past. If anything, I have nothing but respect for how you survived. Too bad you can't cut yourself the same deal."

CHAPTER ELEVEN

THE TUBE IN the neon *e* was burned out, turning the sign into "Fathers." Patience grimaced at the unintentional creepiness.

She wasn't sure what she was doing here. After Stuart left, she'd tried to call Piper back, but her sister didn't pick up, so she'd spent the day sitting on the edge of the bed, replaying Stuart's accusations in her head. She'd spent the night lying in bed doing the same. At first she was angry. How dare he accuse her of having trust issues? Talk about the pot calling the kettle black. Eventually, however, her emotions turned to the important statements. *I love you*. His declaration scared her to death. How could he love her? *Her*. What did the two of them see in her that she didn't see?

When she finally got out of bed, her thoughts led her here. She stared at the broken neon sign wondering if inside held the answers she was looking for.

The front door of Feathers hadn't changed in her absence. The faded black door was still covered with stains, the source of which she never wanted to know, and the beer stench, so strong it seeped through the bricks to reach outside, still made her gag. Familiar as it was, however, she felt as if she was standing in someone else's memory, as if she'd stumbled across an old photograph in a thrift store. Could it be that she'd changed that much in less than a year?

Back when she started at Feathers, she'd had one dream and one dream only: to give Piper a better life. She'd succeeded, too. In fact, she'd go so far as to say she'd done a damn good job. Not only had she given Piper access to a better life, but all of her sister's dreams were coming true.

Did she dare dream a dream for herself now?

Don't let anyone tell you you're not as good as anyone else. How often had she drilled those words into her sister's head? Maybe she'd have done better to drill them into her own.

Stuart loved her. She loved him. She'd probably loved him from the moment he walked through the emergency room doors. Could she trust their love would last?

Then again, two months ago, she hadn't thought love was possible. Not for her, at any rate. She'd started the relationship with Stuart adamant she wouldn't risk her heart and look what happened: she'd fallen in love, anyway. Being with him had made her feel special. And if she could feel that good while believing their relationship to be a fantasy, how good might she feel if she opened her heart to it completely?

"Well, will you look who's come back." Like a miniskirt-wearing gift that kept on giving, Chablis ambled around the corner. She had a cigarette in her hand. Smoke break. Patience always did find it laughable that taking their clothes off was okay but smoking inside was against the law.

The dancer tapped ash onto the sidewalk. "What's the matter? Boyfriend dump your stuck-up behind?" she asked, before taking a long drag.

Smoke filtered through her magenta-lined lips. Guess you ain't better than us, after all?"

"You know what, Chablis...?" Patience paused. A week ago—even a day ago—Patience might have thrown Chablis's smack talk back in her face. She no longer felt the need. Chablis was stuck in a world Patience no longer belonged in.

"You're right. I'm not better than you. I'm not better than anybody." She smiled. "But I'm no worse, either."

Since Patience didn't expect the dancer to understand what she was saying, it wasn't a surprise when Chablis's face wrinkled in confusion. "Whatever." She reached for the door handle.

Through the gap, Patience saw the dimly lit scenery from a lifetime ago. Once again, it was like looking at someone else's photograph. Stuart was right—Feathers was in her past. The future was what she dared to make of it. That was something else she used to tell Piper. *Don't be afraid to go for your dreams.* High time she took her own advice.

And this time, she was going to do without lying or hiding from who she was. Stuart said he loved the real her? Well, the real her was who he was going to get.

"Excuse me, miss?"

The male voice startled her. Stiffening, she turned, expecting to find a customer. Instead, she came face-to-face with a young police officer.

He gave her an apologetic smile. "Is everything all right? You look lost."

If he only knew. "I was," she told him, "but I think I know where I'm going now."

"Do you need directions? Trust me, you don't want to go in there. It's no place for a lady."

Patience looked at the closed door of her past. "You're right," she agreed. "I think I'd much rather go home."

"You can't manage without a housekeeper," Stuart told Ana. They were having a lousy excuse for breakfast—his version of scrambled eggs and coffee—in the kitchen. Or rather he was. Pieces of Ana's eggs somehow kept landing on the floor for Nigel to eat. She'd been protesting his cooking the past three days. "What will you do when I move out?"

"You could stay."

"Sure." They'd had this argument before, too. "How about I adopt a cat and name her Patience, too. People won't talk."

He knew why his aunt was dragging her feet. She was hoping Patience would change her mind and come back. Stuart hoped she'd come home, too, but he was a realist. It'd been three days since he poured his heart out in Patience's motel room. Three days since he said he loved her. And they hadn't heard a word. Whether he wanted it to or not, life had to go on.

The doorbell rang. "That's the candidate from the employment agency. I'll go get her. Try to keep an open mind," he said.

"If an open mind means telling her no, then fine, I'll keep an open mind."

Rolling his eyes, Stuart left the kitchen, Nigel chasing after him. "I hope you're planning on being cooperative," he told the cat. Otherwise, this was going to be a long morning. He opened the front door…

And froze in place.

On the threshold stood Patience, dressed for work in her blue work shirt and capris. In her hands, she held a feather duster. "Rumor has it you need a housekeeper."

She was back. The hopefulness behind her smile made him want to pull her into his arms then and there, but he resisted. This was her decision; he needed to let her play it out her way.

He settled then for smiling. "Did the employment agency send you over."

"No. I'm just a woman who's made a lot of mistakes looking to start over. I don't suppose there's a place for someone like me here?"

"Oh, there is." He pushed the front door wide. "Come on in. There's a little old lady in the kitchen who's going to be thrilled to meet you."

"Just her?"

"Me, too."

"Good." She smiled. "Although I should warn

you in advance. I'm very much in love with this lawyer I know."

Stuart's heart gave a tiny victory cheer. "Sounds like a lucky guy."

"I'm the lucky one. Like I said, I made a lot of mistakes, and am hoping he—you—will give me a second chance."

Now he gave in and pulled her close, kissing her with everything in his heart. "You don't have to ask twice," he told her.

Patience wrapped her arms around his waist. To Stuart it felt that she was afraid he'd disappear. "I'm sorry I didn't trust you," she said into his chest.

"Same here. This time we'll trust each other."

"That's a new thing for me—to trust someone. I might stumble a little bit." She looked up, her eyes as bright as the brightest chocolate diamond in the world. "Will you be patient with me?"

"Patient with Patience?" Grinning at his lame joke, he kissed the top of her head. "I don't think that's going to be a problem. Both of us are going to screw up, sweetheart. But as far as I'm concerned we've got all the time in the world to teach each other. Forever even."

Her arms squeezed tighter. The word *forever* was scaring her, he knew. Someday it wouldn't, though. Someday she'd realize she was so loved that forever was the only possible time frame.

"Forever sounds like a good goal," she said finally, her bravery increasing the admiration he held for her. "I love you, Stuart Duchenko."

He'd never believed three words more. They'd get to forever. He knew they would. "I love you too. Now…" Giving her a reluctant last kiss, he shut the door. "How about we go make an old lady's day?"

A meow sounded at his feet. "You, too, Nigel."

Together, the three walked toward the future.

Two weeks later

"Why is the phone ringing in the middle of the night?" Stuart groaned. "Don't they realize we're tired?"

"Poor baby. They probably don't realize how

hard furniture shopping was for you." Patience grinned at the pout she spied before he covered his head with his pillow. The two of them and Ana had spent the day shopping for Stuart's new condominium. He was scheduled to move out at the end of the week. Ana was disappointed, until she learned Patience would be staying put. For now. As madly as they loved each other, both she and Stuart decided they should take their relationship one step at a time. Eventually, Patience would move in, but for now, there was no need to rush. Like Stuart said. They had forever.

Forever was such a nice-sounding word. Patience believed in it a little more every day. Turned out Prince Charming not only walked through the door, but he stuck around, as well.

"Whoever it is, tell them they're insane," Stuart muttered from beneath his pillow. "Then get under these covers so I can do unspeakable things to you."

"I thought you were sleepy?" she whispered, snatching the phone off the end table.

A hand snaked around to splay against her bare abdomen. "I'm awake now."

She answered without bothering to suppress her giggle. There was only one person who'd call at this hour and she wouldn't care. "Piper?"

"Greetings from England." There was a pause. "I'm not interrupting something, am I?"

"Not yet." She slapped Stuart's roaming hand. "What are you doing in England?"

"Helping your boyfriend, of course. And I have good news, and more good news. Which one do you want first?"

"Start with the good news."

"We found Ana's painting."

"You did!" She sat up. "That's wonderful."

"That's why we're in England. The gallery in Paris gave us a lead on a collector here who purchased one of Nigel's paintings. Turns out, the painting is of Ana. Almost identical to the one in the background of the picture Stuart emailed."

Seemed silly to be moved to tears over a nude painting, but Patience's eyes started to water.

After all these years, Ana was finally getting a piece of her Nigel back. "Ana is going to be so thrilled when she hears the news."

Hearing his aunt's name, Stuart immediately sat up, too, and mouthed the word *painting*? Patience nodded. He pressed a kiss to her cheek.

"Even better, the owner is willing to sell. Tell Stuart I'll email him the name and contact information."

"Thank you so much for doing this, Piper." Ana meant so much to her and Stuart. That they could finally reclaim this piece of her past was but small repayment. "Thank Frederic, as well."

"I will. Now, do you want the other good news?"

Patience looked at the man sitting next to her, feeling overwhelmed with good fortune. She didn't think it was possible for life to get better. However, Piper certainly sounded happy, so she was definitely curious. "Yes. What's the other good news?"

"Well…" There was a long dramatic pause before her sister finally replied.

"I got married."

She nearly dropped the phone. "Did you say married?" How? When? *Who?*

"It's a long story," Piper said. "Do you have time?"

Was she kidding? For news like this, Patience had all the time in the world. "I couldn't hang up now if I tried." She settled back to hear what her baby sister had to say.

By the end of Piper's story, Patience had tears in her eyes. Stuart was right there, his strong arms ready to provide solace. "You going to be okay?" he asked, when she hung up the phone.

"She did it," Patience whispered. "Everything I ever dreamed for her. She did it." Her heart felt so full she thought it might burst.

One of her tears escaped. Stuart brushed the moisture from her cheek and she smiled, thinking about their first night on the roof. "I was so certain Piper would be the only one of us to find love and have a happy ending."

"And now?"

She shifted in his arms, so she could look into

the eyes of the man who'd captured her heart the moment he walked through the hospital door. "Now, it looks like I was wrong. Because I can't imagine a happier ending than being with you."

* * * * *

If you loved this book and want to enjoy Piper's story too, watch out for BEAUTY & HER BILLIONAIRE BOSS by Barbara Wallace, available in January 2016!